DUNBAR'S FOLLY AND OTHER STORIES

DUNBAR'S FOLLY AND OTHER STORIES

Matthew Duffus

TABLE OF CONTENTS

ENJOY YOUR STAY

Fourteen months after his wife's sentencing, Eli met the stepdaughter he hadn't known existed. This happened in mid-April, when business slowed, the winter-sports crowd gone with the melted snow, the summer season months away, so he reserved his finest room for her. He aired it himself, changing the linen on the queen-sized bed, stocking the fireplace, the last operable one outside of the parlor, with wood he'd split expressly for this purpose, dusting the bureau and the wardrobe, even washing the long window overlooking Mariner's meager downtown. To the east, he could see Lake Superior, two blocks away, through the gaps in the buildings. The stepdaughter, Marlene, lived in Chicago. He worried she'd find his inn hokey, but nothing could be done about that; after three generations and eighty-five years without closing, not for the 1932 flood or the more routine blizzards and ice storms, the Mariner Inn existed outside of history and the fads that had absorbed so much of its now-defunct competition. At least he liked to think so.

Marlene arrived on a Thursday, as he served afternoon tea to the inn's lone guests, an academic couple from the Twin Cities. The bell jangled, and then stopped abruptly when a draft slammed shut the door, rattling the windows. Eli paused, listening to the interloper's clopping footsteps on the hardwood floor. The steps rang out, slow and even, and by the time he'd served the tea and kringla, she stood in the doorway. She was tall and striking, like her mother, with spiky auburn hair. Freckles dotted her cheeks and the upturned nose that twitched as she looked around. Younger than he'd expected, mid-twenties, she had the air of someone at home under any circumstances. She dropped her duffle bag and shrugged off a backpack, taking her time unbuttoning her form-fitting gray trench coat before entering the room.

"You must be Eli," she said, ignoring the inquisitive eyes of the middle-aged couple who seemed to sense that, at last, something interesting might happen.

He bowed to the couple and said, "Please excuse me," before taking Marlene's outstretched hand. Her grip was firm, confident, though she had trouble maintaining eye contact. When she did look at him, he felt dizzy. She had her mother's eyes, both their size—verging on being too large for her face—and their cool blue color.

They didn't speak while he led her upstairs to the room, and he remained silent, in the doorway, while she walked the perimeter, like a cat, before taking the bags from him and heaving them onto the bed. The springs creaked, and she turned to him. "This is a good mattress, right? I can't sleep on one that isn't firm." In her voice he heard the same insistent tone she'd had when she'd first called, five weeks earlier. "She's in prison? What did she do?" No shock, no utterances of denial or feigned disbelief.

Not knowing what to say, he stuck to what they had in common. "Have you spoken to your mother?"

"I saw her on my way up here, like I told you." She dropped onto the bed, slinging one foot beneath her. By the lack of a reaction, he figured it met her standards.

"That's right." She'd told him she was going to stop at the prison. "I'm having trouble getting my head around this. I don't know why Joyce never mentioned you."

"She left without any warning when I was fourteen, so forgive me if I don't share your surprise. That's how she is. Secretive."

"So I'm learning."

"She told me you haven't visited her much."

"It's five hours each way. Someone has to manage things here."

"Guess that's why you two get along."

"Excuse me?"

"You're both good at cutting people out."

"I was in court every day for weeks. And I visited once a month, in the beginning. I'm sorry she left you, but I had nothing to do with it."

"You weren't her landing pad when she left Chicago?"

"If I was, I didn't know it any better than you did."

She gave him a long look with her mother's eyes. It was all he could do not to swoon. He gripped the doorframe behind him with both hands and waited for Marlene to look away. She didn't. But the bell at the front desk dinged, giving him an excuse to leave. He stopped on the landing to regain his composure. Time to pretend he was still the unflappable owner of a four-star hotel.

*

Twelve years earlier, Eli's future wife had arrived in the lobby of the Mariner Inn without a reservation, fortunate that news of a freak Columbus Day snowstorm had sent his timid, Fall-foliage-studying guests south the day before. The inn wouldn't remain empty for long; he had spent the afternoon fielding calls from enthusiasts who wanted to be the first to break through the predicted foot of snow on their cross-country skis. So close to the Boundary Waters with Canada, where motorized vehicles were prohibited, he relied on such clientele to make it through the winter, knowing the hardcore among them would be back once a month through March.

He was answering one such call when he heard the front door open. He assumed it was the mail carrier or a local businessperson come to chat about the weather, so he didn't look up right away. When he did, he saw a woman shivering before him, her thin jacket and dark hair covered with snow, two bulky suitcases at her side like extensions of her arms.

"The storm—" Her teeth chattered as she spoke. "My car got stuck. I walked."

"Wait there." He hurried into the office and grabbed a stack of towels still warm from the dryer. "Give me your coat," he said once he'd returned.

She obeyed, like a small child, and he dried her hair, frizzy with static, wrapped a second towel around her shoulders, and bent down to remove her loafers. She shifted from foot to foot, and he could feel how cold she was through her socks.

"How long were you walking?"

"Forty-five minutes? An hour? The roads were fine when I left Duluth."

He led her to a room, drew a hot bath, and left her alone, without exchanging names, itineraries, or billing information. Owning an inn had taught him to mix polite, informal chit chat with the business of credit card numbers and room deposits, but he could tell, in this case, that more pressing matters existed. This woman was so out of her element that he felt the need to take care of her, even though he'd put her in a room he'd already reserved for a loyal, snowshoeing guest. He'd worry about that later.

By the time she descended the stairs an hour later, Eli had notified his seasonal staff that he'd need help beginning that evening and transferred the phone to voicemail so he could prepare for the unexpected rush. Fall and spring were the slow periods, when he typically got by with a skeleton crew, and while he'd hoped to carry on this way until November, he could use the extra business. But instead of seeing to the rest of the laundry, double-checking the kitchen's provisions, or restocking toiletries, he sat in the parlor with his lone guest.

"I don't mean to be a burden," she said, even as she sat content to watch him stoke the fire, fluff the pillows on either end of her love seat, and pour her a cup of tea from his grandmother's service. She shivered after accepting the cup, Earl Grey sloshing onto the saucer.

"You're still cold."

"Just a chill." She looked down at her hand, at the liquid dribbling down her long, slender fingers. "A little drafty in here."

"All part of the charm."

"Have you been here long?"

"It was my grandparents' originally. What about you? Here for long?"

Outside, chunky snowflakes clung to the windows, blown by the wind that rustled the remaining leaves on the trees. She watched the snow for a few moments, even after the wind had died down, and then said, "Must be nice to feel so rooted. I get restless."

They carried on this way, Eli asking questions at first out of politeness—most guests loved to talk about themselves and where they were from—and then out of a sense of increasing curiosity as she dodged, deflected, and ignored his queries. After half an hour, he'd learned her name, Joyce Deaton, and that she'd been hired as the new orthopedist at the hospital twenty miles away, though her apartment wouldn't be available for several days.

"I couldn't wait any longer," she said, as close to an explanation as she'd yet offered. "It was time to go."

Before he could respond, a station wagon pulled into the loading zone, a phalanx of skis strapped to its roof.

The driver, a regular who'd been coming almost as long as Eli had been running the inn, honked and waved, a toothy smile peeking through a thick gray beard. The man threw his hands into the air, approvingly, as though saying, What great luck! Eli rose. The rush had begun.

*

Babette's Feast, the restaurant beneath the inn, had been open seven years, long enough to be featured in *Minnesota Monthly* and *Gourmet* and, as a result, to build a following among the locals and as a destination for traveling foodies, but on the night of Marlene's arrival, it hosted only four patrons: the academics from the inn and a young couple from nearby Grand Marais, whom Eli saw on a weekly basis. Soon after he and Marlene seated themselves and opened their menus, Suzanne, the owner, appeared from the kitchen, chef's coat splattered with sauces and smeared handprints. She smiled at the other guests on her way to Eli's table, where she sat down heavily, bouncing against the chair's bottom.

After Eli made the introductions, Marlene tapped the closed menu with her forefinger. "Your food's French, but *Babette's Feast* was Danish, wasn't it?"

Suzanne groaned. "People ask that all the time. Babette, herself, was French, along with most of what she prepared for the feast."

"Are the mushrooms fresh? I used to work in fine dining. I can't stand frozen or canned *anything*."

"Neither can I," Suzanne said. "If it isn't fresh, it isn't on the menu."

"Then I'll have the mushroom *Vol-au-Vent*."

Suzanne smiled at her and said, "I'll tell your waiter." She turned to Eli, arched an eyebrow, and slapped her hand against her thigh. "I better get back. Save room for dessert. I just made profiteroles."

Alone again, Marlene said, "No offense, but why would someone open a French restaurant here? You don't even have a McDonalds."

"Maybe that's why. Everyone prefers *roulade* and..." he looked at the menu— "*saumon à l'oseille*. She should know. She grew up here, came back to open this place after she got tired of living in France."

"Poor thing."

"You think this is out of the way, you should hear about some of the places where she worked."

Marlene frowned and picked up the wine list. "What's good?"

"I don't drink anymore. But I always liked the *Chateauneuf du Pape*."

"A little pricey."

"It's on me."

Only after they'd eaten, Marlene picking at her puff pastry, Eli attacking his rabbit with a relish intended to spur her on, did he bring up Joyce directly. "How was your mother?"

"I don't have much to compare her to, but I didn't seen any shiv scars or gang tattoos."

"You must have an opinion."

She poured the last of the wine and swirled her glass around, studying the color in the candlelight. "We spent most of our time talking about you, actually."

"So you're here to check up on me?"

She downed the wine. "I don't feel much like banter. I'm just trying to put the last fifteen years back together."

Before he could respond, Suzanne arrived with their desserts, two shallow bowls with four pastries each, cut in half and filled with vanilla ice cream covered in a thick chocolate sauce, and topped with almond shavings. A dessert fit for a last meal, he'd told her the first time she'd made it for him and Joyce, to celebrate their eighth wedding anniversary. Suzanne looked from Eli to Marlene and back again. He could tell she wanted to say something but limited herself to, "*Bon appetit.*"

"She likes you," Marlene said when they were alone.

"We grew up together. She worked upstairs when we were in high school."

"No," she said, slicing her spoon through one of the pastries. "She likes you. I can tell."

*

When Joyce finally left the Mariner Inn, after three weeks, it wasn't to move into an apartment but into Eli's house next door. It had been his grandparents' place, a two-story brownstone that abutted the inn, with a

15

connecting door through the laundry that he'd had sealed off when he inherited it. At the time, he'd thought that while the inn was his job, it didn't have to be his life.

He'd been so nervous about inviting Joyce to live with him that her ready acceptance surprised him more than a rejection would have. In the past, he had smothered women with too much attention too early, and while he feared he was doing the same once again, he couldn't help himself. They'd made love Joyce's third day in Mariner, begun spending the night together two evenings later, growing so entwined that Joyce often answered the office phone for him. When she began at the hospital, after a week, he found himself adrift during the hours she was gone, a feeling he hadn't experienced since he had been a much younger man. His life had become self-contained, defined by his work and the occasional visit from the few school friends still in the area. For the most part, he was content to work himself to exhaustion, go to bed, and start the process all over again.

Joyce changed that. She encouraged him to hire more staff, to take entire days off for trips to state parks or languorous afternoons on Artist's Point, where they watched the ships and drank thermoses of coffee. Early on, she even spoke of buying a boat, an expense they decided to forego in favor of renovating the inn's basement when Suzanne moved back to care for her ailing parents. Eli reasoned that a fine dining establishment was the one missing piece that would put the inn on the map. Though Joyce had disagreed, she acknowledged, years later, when the inn was advertising in a dozen national periodicals, that it had been the right thing to do.

He had never been married before, and Joyce claimed she hadn't been, but though Eli pushed for them to set a date, she was hesitant.

"What will it change?" she said. "Aren't we happy right now? I'm too old for kids, so we don't have that as an excuse."

"It's worth it for the symbolism. I want to make public—"

"Then announce how you feel to all your guests, I don't care. I just don't know why we have to label it and put it behind glass."

"I'm not talking about a museum piece."

"More like mounting a butterfly."

"That's a bit dramatic," he said.

"I'm not the one who wants to get dressed up to take part in some spectacle."

They'd gone round and round like this for months before Joyce had given in, out of the blue. Now, Eli wondered if she had needed time to settle her affairs in Chicago. From everything Marlene said, her mother had fled town like someone in witness protection.

The ceremony had taken place on a cool November Saturday, a little over a year after Joyce arrived in town. They were married by a justice of the peace, at Joyce's insistence, on the patio behind their house, with only twenty people in attendance, including Eli's mother, in one of her final forays away from home. Joyce wore an antique lavender gown with a matching cashmere wrap to guard against the chill, and he overdid it in a rented morning suit. I'll only get married once, he reasoned as he buttoned the wool waistcoat. His mother cried, he fought back tears of his own, and Joyce looked so serious that only a handful of pictures captured her smiling.

*

Eli rolled over when he felt the mattress shift. Marlene had been at the inn for four days before he'd decided it was safe for Suzanne to spend the night. Even though he still lived next door, he hadn't wanted to risk the two women running into each other, at least not until he'd discovered that Marlene showed no interest in leaving. He didn't want to be rude, so he hadn't asked about her plans, but he got the sense he was in for an extended visit.

"Sorry to wake you," Suzanne said. She smelled of soap and body lotion, with the faintest trace of raw onion in the background. When she curled up next to him, he enfolded her in his arms.

"I was waiting for you," he said.

They'd begun seeing each other, tentatively, several months earlier, almost a year into his wife's eight-year sentence. For once, Eli had taken things slowly, though not out of fear of discovery. During his wife's troubles, he'd learned how much of an outsider she'd remained, even after so many years in Mariner. Friends, business associates, and locals stopped by to ask after him, to offer him their support, but no one mentioned his wife, as though he'd lost her permanently. Under the circumstances, he doubted anyone would fault him for taking comfort in Suzanne's affections, and even if they did, Midwestern reticence would keep them quiet. No, he'd decided to move slowly owing to how right it felt being with Suzanne. He'd known her longer than anyone in his life, didn't have to go through the pitfalls and landmines of the getting-accustomed stage. They already shared a frame of reference, a language of intimacy, and his feelings for her frightened him enough that he remained on guard, not wanting to carry their relationship too far too quickly.

Around the time Marlene first called, they'd begun spending most nights together, at his place. The backyards of the two buildings connected, so it was easy for Suzanne to enter through his kitchen door and take the stairs to his warm bed after a long day at work. He always waited up for her.

"How is she?" Suzanne said, burrowing deeper into him.

"I don't know how she fills her days. She doesn't hike, rarely leaves the hotel, has turned down my offer to loan her books."

"Conserving her energy for mealtime. That girl can *eat*."

After the first night, she'd begun devouring everything put before her, including two starters, a main dish, and dessert each night at dinner. "She's going to bankrupt me."

"You never should have started paying for her."

"I know the chef. I keep hoping she can be persuaded to offer a discount."

"Really." Her hand slid down his stomach and between his legs, grasping him through his pajama bottoms. "Do you have anything to offer in return?"

Later, after Suzanne had fallen asleep, her breathing deep and nasally, he slipped out of bed and walked downstairs. He still felt guilty for being with someone other than his wife, but after all the secrets she'd kept, it was difficult to feel too badly at the betrayal. At least he felt that way when he was alone. Having Marlene next door increased his guilt significantly. Even after so many years, the pain from her mother's abandonment was close to the surface. He wondered if Joyce would feel the same way if she knew about Suzanne. Unlike her daughter, she'd never shown the least concern when Suzanne moved back to town. "You're old friends," she'd say whenever Eli felt the need to apologize for spending so much time with her. "No explanation needed."

In the kitchen, he poured a glass of water, drank it in one gulp, and then chastised himself. Even if he did fall asleep, he'd be up in an hour to use the bathroom. The joys of a sixty-year-old prostate. Suzanne had left a tray of profiteroles in the refrigerator, and he ate three of them, one after the other, so mechanically he barely paused to enjoy them. He'd gained seven pounds since they'd been together. He'd have to start exercising again if this was to continue.

Upstairs, he turned left, into the guest room, instead of continuing down the hallway and back to his bedroom. He didn't want to bother Suzanne with his tossing and turning, his trips to the bathroom, so he slipped into the guest bed and picked up the book he'd left on the nightstand a week earlier, the last time insomnia had visited him. He'd read ninety pages that night. One or two more such nights and he'd know who'd killed Roger Ackroyd.

*

When the police had called, he'd been salting the front walk. An accident between Mariner and Grand Marais. One fatality, though not his wife, thank God. He barely took the time to put away his supplies before heading to the hospital, where he found Joyce in remarkably good condition, under the circumstances. She had abrasions on her nose and forehead from the airbag, a dislocated shoulder, and a sprained knee. She wouldn't even need surgery, unlike the surviving victim, who spent hours having his spine fused in an effort to allow him to walk again.

"What happened?" he asked once he knew his wife was all right.

"I misjudged the distance, clipped the car's back end when I made the turn onto 68. I wonder if they braked for some reason. I was sure they'd already gone past." Both cars spun out on the ice, but only one tumbled down the embankment and into the scrub.

A sheriff's deputy entered the room, looking both stern and uncomfortable. Once he'd introduced himself, he said, "I know this is bad timing, but we're going to have to do a Breathalyzer."

"That's overkill, don't you think," Eli said. "My wife made a mistake in the snow. She's hardly drunk." It had happened before eight in the morning, when both cars were on their way to work.

"I can get a warrant to test her blood if you won't cooperate."

"On what grounds?"

"It's all right, Eli," Joyce said. "He's doing his job."

"I'd like to know why you're being treated this way. Will the other driver be tested?" She'd never been good in the snow, always deferred to him whenever they drove anywhere together.

"You want to know?" the deputy said, hooking his thumbs in his gun belt and puffing out his chest. "The water bottle in Dr. Sundberg's cup holder was filled—half filled—with vodka."

"She doesn't drink—"

"Enough," Joyce said. "I'll take the damn test."

Even two hours after the accident, she was close to three times the legal limit. She didn't deny it, seemed defiant, if anything, refusing to enter rehab as an attempt at leniency. "I killed that poor woman," she told Eli and her lawyer. "I should go to prison." The jury offered no sympathy to a drunk doctor on her way to work, and even Eli's reserves dried up as he found more alcohol stashed around the house, in her mangled car, and hidden in her office. The more he saw his wife before the trial, the more he began to wonder if this was the first time he'd been around a sober Joyce; she was irritable and morose, in keeping with the reality of the situation, but also cold, distant, refusing affection or comfort. She'd put up a barrier between herself and the world, one that kept even her husband out.

While she maintained her perfect posture every day during the trial, he found each one progressively more difficult, the recounting of details, the character witnesses who catalogued her slips and unreliability, the sad presence of the mourning, wheelchair-bound widower. It was almost enough to drive him to drink.

Instead, he threw himself into his work, repainting rooms, re-grouting bathroom floors, pressure-washing the inn's exterior, anything that would leave him exhausted enough to sleep at the end of the day. Suzanne looked after him, cooking lunch and dinner, insisting he keep on enough staff to take one day off each week, and then forcing him out of the house on those dull Mondays, driving him to Duluth in an attempt to take his mind off his troubles. It hadn't worked, not at first, but by the time Joyce began her sentence, he'd found himself looking forward to their excursions, no matter how guilty he felt for doing so.

He wasn't sure any more which of them had made the first move, only that it felt right when it happened. They were walking back to the car, having spent an hour wandering around downtown Duluth after dinner, when they found themselves in a clinch, kissing tentatively at first, soon growing hungry for each other. After that first time, a hurried affair in Suzanne's station wagon, they'd backed off, to make sure they were doing what they both really wanted.

At the same time, his trips to the correctional facility in Shakopee grew less frequent. He refused to blame this on Suzanne. Each visit left him in a funk for days, between Joyce's reticence and the depressing spectacle of his fellow visitors, many of them families who clamored for their inmate's attention, took group photos, and shared home-cooked meals, when allowed. Meanwhile, he and Joyce sat across from each other, increasingly silent, rarely making eye contact even when they did talk.

If the growing gap between his visits bothered her, she never let on to him.

※

A week into the visit, with no sign of an endpoint in sight, Marlene began helping at the inn. They never discussed it or worked out an arrangement; one day she stopped Eli on his way to make afternoon tea and said she'd do it.

"Don't let it steep too long. Dr. Kirkland—"

"I know how to make tea," she said, patting his arm. It was the first time they'd touched since she'd shaken his hand on her arrival.

Still, he watched from the hallway as she served the Kirklands and the Lloyds, their newest guests. She poured the tea without spilling a drop and sliced the tea ring expertly. The tiny kitchen behind the office smelled of cardamom long after he'd baked it, and though he'd looked forward to impressing Mrs. Kirkland, he was pleased to see Marlene taking an interest.

Over the next few days, she began covering front desk duties during the afternoon, once she emerged from her room, sitting with a book that she read in between accepting reservations and fielding questions from the Lloyds, who had turned out to be his most demanding guests in months, constantly in need of fresh linens, a recommendation for a new place for lunch, or a breathtaking vista for their afternoon strolls. From the office, Eli could hear Marlene answer each query without once growing impatient.

On the third day of their informal arrangement, she appeared in the office doorway a half hour before tea, which she'd continued serving, and cleared her throat, waiting for him to look up. He'd been lost in thought, designing a new quarter-page magazine advertisement, and needed a few moments to refocus his attention.

Once he had, Marlene said, "I could manage here for a day or two if you want to visit my mother."

"That's all right," he said. "I don't want to inconvenience you."

"When was the last time you were there?"

"I have so much to do. This place will be packed in a few weeks, once everything is properly thawed."

"I know. I've been taking the reservations. Even more reason to go now, while you can."

He looked at the computer screen. The font was all wrong. He'd aimed for classic and missed the mark. It looked fussy instead.

"My mother said you haven't been since New Year's."

"You're checking up on me?"

"She misses you."

"She said that?"

"Not exactly." Marlene picked at the door frame with one of her long, manicured nails. "You don't want to go," she said.

"It's complicated."

"Isn't everything?"

"If I try to explain, will you stop doing that?"

She came forward and sat in the chair opposite the desk, crossed her legs and arms, and waited for him to continue.

"You know how you felt when your mother left? I'm still in a place not far off from there."

"Don't treat me like a child," she said.

"She killed someone. Isn't that enough?"

"Maybe for some people. But you work yourself to the bone to keep the family business going, and you said it yourself, you were in court every day. You're loyal, to a fault. But now..."

"You think my loyalties have shifted?"

"I think they're misplaced."

"What's the difference?"

"Go down there and find out for yourself."

He mentioned the conversation to Suzanne that night. They were in bed, post-coital, and she shifted onto her side to look at him, propping herself on one arm. Even in the dark, he knew she was searching his face for signs of how he felt.

Once she'd given up, she said, "You're going, aren't you?"

"Do I have a choice? She already suspects something's going on."

"So tell her the truth." When he didn't respond, she added, "You're afraid Joyce will find out."

"*When* Joyce finds out, it'll be my choice. I'm not going to be forced into it by anyone."

She ran a hand through the hair on his bare thigh, and then patted his leg. "I know this isn't easy."

"For either of us."

They were both silent so long he figured she'd fallen asleep. But right before he was about to get up and go to the kitchen, Suzanne said, "Don't worry about me. I'm here, aren't I?"

He wrapped his arms around her, pulling her close, and remained that way, listening to the light snoring that began ten minutes later, putting up with the pins and needles in his shoulder and the insomnia that kept him awake until after three. When he finally drifted off, it was to images of the long trip south, down the same road Joyce had crashed on, past Duluth, where he'd spent so many illicit days with Suzanne, through the broad expanses on either side of I-35, and into the Twin Cities. He had the route memorized, knew how long it would take and where he would stop for gas. He knew everything except what he'd say to Joyce when he finally saw her again.

*

No matter how many times he'd been there, he couldn't get used to how unlike a prison the facility looked. The brick buildings, with plenty of windows, and manicured landscaping reminded him of a college campus, not a correctional facility. Even the inmates, all women, in gray or blue sweat suits, looked harmless. Looks can be deceiving, he knew. The prison held one hundred killers at any time, his wife among them.

Eli waited for Joyce, who was allowed contact visits, in the waiting room, remaining seated in his assigned spot when the door opened, and she was admitted into the room. She had on heavy khakis with a blue sweatshirt tucked into the waistband. Her hair was longer than he'd ever seen it, hanging limply to her shoulders. Its grayness still surprised him. Until the trial, she'd had it dyed every month, without fail. Now it was the color of steel wool.

They were permitted one hug and a kiss on the cheek when she entered, but though Eli stood up to greet her, he could tell she wasn't interested in state-sanctioned intimacy. Instead, she sat down, careful to keep her hands in her lap, in view of the guards. A year earlier, they used to get in trouble for reaching out for each other, instinctively, while they talked. They'd since learned the appropriate behavior.

"I thought it must have been a mistake when they told me you were here. I told the CO, 'My husband is *too busy* to visit me.'"

"I'm sorry," he said. They were five feet apart, and for the first time in months, he wished he could break the rules, touch her in some—any—way.

"Of course you are. You're always sorry. My cellmate's husband brings their kids every other week. They even have their picture taken together."

"Like you and Marlene?"

She smiled, the scowl on her face brightening momentarily. "I didn't think she'd go through with it."

"She's been in Mariner twelve days now."

"She's determined."

"She's interested in your—our—life."

"Is that what she told you?" She smiled again, this one even brighter than the first one.

Joyce always seemed to have an agenda when he visited, turning their conversations into a game of chess between two opponents, one of whom hadn't yet mastered checkers. He waited for her to continue, knowing anything he said could be dismissed or send her over the edge, cutting short the visit.

"She's known where I lived all along. When she was a kid, her father wouldn't let her visit. Until recently, she had no interest in disobeying him."

"Meaning?"

She leaned forward, resting her elbows on her knees, and then sat up straight again when the visiting room officer cleared her throat. She ran her hands along her khakis, the dry skin of her palms rasping against the heavy-duty fabric.

"My office address was on every check I sent. Phone number, too. But she didn't care about either of those until the money stopped coming."

"I don't follow."

"Do you really think a judge let me disappear from her life that easily? Ever heard of child support?"

"She's an adult now."

"How about penance?"

"You're saying she's after money?"

"And I thought I'd have to draw you a picture. She told me she'd contact you if I didn't find a way to restart the payments."

"Blackmail?"

She smiled again. Eli was beginning to hate the way she did this, as though she were condescending to a slow-witted child.

"That sounds dramatic. But not far off." She looked around. "Is she with you? I'd love to see her face now that she knows it won't work."

"She's covering for me at the inn."

"Oh, Eli. You always were gullible."

"Why should I believe you?"

"What point would there be in me lying to you now?"

He thought about Marlene, about how long it had taken her to grow comfortable around him, at the inn, about the help she'd been providing, free of charge. Was she capable of the con job her mother seemed to think she was running? Try as he might, he couldn't see it.

"Forgive me if I don't accept your words at face value."

"Your mistake," she said.

From the parking lot, he tried Suzanne's cell and the phone in her kitchen but got no answer. He didn't want to leave what Joyce had told him on her voicemail, felt foolish for giving it any credence whatsoever, so he hung up and pulled out of the lot. Five hours might be long enough for him to figure out how he felt about what he'd heard.

*

When he returned to Mariner, having shaved twenty minutes off his time, he found the first floor empty. The guests were in their rooms, the fireplace dark, the front desk empty. Marlene rarely stayed past dinner, but with him gone, he'd imagined she might. She'd washed the dishes from afternoon tea, left them in the draining board in the kitchenette, and switched the phones to voicemail. The Mariner Inn was a full-service establishment, but guests so rarely needed anything after nine P.M. that he gave them his cell number instead of hiring someone to work the night shift.

He still hadn't been able to reach Suzanne, and when he walked downstairs to the restaurant, he remembered why. Wednesday was half-priced wine night, the busiest service of the week during the off months. Even at ten, the room was three-quarters-full of locals enjoying pan roasted poussin with Brussels sprouts, truffled pecorino, or dulcey mousse with hazelnut sponge. Suzanne had transformed the entire area into foodies.

The kitchen door swung open and Marlene appeared, carrying two plates of brown butter panna cotta, a dish too rich even for Eli. She was dressed in black with a white apron tied at her waist, the official Babette's Feast attire. She walked quickly, though her upper body remained still, all of the action happening from the waist down. Her spiky hair had been tamed, somewhat, and she smiled freely as she delivered the plates to the local dentist and his wife.

Eli thought about what his wife had told him. Was this woman really the shakedown artist Joyce claimed her to be? Was she now conning him, and Suzanne? Or was Joyce still only giving him part of the story? Early in her sentence, he'd confronted her about all of the alcohol he'd found—the case of water bottles filled with vodka, the half-gallon jugs hidden behind the cleaning supplies, the Tupperwares full of the stuff on the higher shelves in the garage—only to find himself stonewalled, practically laughed at. "So I have a problem," she'd said. "Do you really need more confirmation?" He couldn't help feeling that with Marlene, she'd left another problem behind.

He continued watching from the doorway. Even crowded, the dining room held thirty, at most, and she handled the tables with ease. Most of the diners had progressed to dessert, though the wine continued to flow liberally into their glasses. He'd seen enough, he decided. He would talk to Suzanne later. But before he could leave, the kitchen door opened again, and she emerged in her chef's whites. She stopped next to Marlene, at the server's station, and laughed at something the younger woman said. They turned, in unison, to survey the room, and when she saw him in the doorway, she put a hand on Marlene's arm and mouthed what looked like, *I'm keeping her.*

He shrugged and left before Marlene could notice him watching her. He'd turned off the lights on the way downstairs, not expecting to return, and was careful on the uneven stone steps. Though he'd been walking this route for years, he tested each stair before he placed his full weight on it. The last thing he needed, so late in the day, was an accident.

DUNBAR'S FOLLY

As soon as Provost Nickerson asked him what he intended to do in his retirement, George Dunbar knew he was in trouble. *Transformation* was the new watch word: out with the old and in with the less expensive. He'd seen it happen to Bob Toback, in Music, and to the English Department's Medievalist, Sheri Albertson. But they were both practically seventy while he was a mere sixty-four, a wonderful age, numerically speaking. It was even, which he liked, and the product of eight-squared, four-cubed, or two-to-the-sixth-power, which pleased him to no end. He kept these numerical predilections to himself and countered the provost's buy-out offer with a statement of fact.

"You and I are the same age, David. When will you be transformed?"

The provost smiled, predictably—the man was known for the fifty-seven varieties of his smiles—and said, "My position adds value to my age, whereas you..." Nickerson dropped any pretense of enjoying the conversation. "This is the best offer you'll receive," he said. "And it comes with a very narrow window."

That afternoon, Dunbar accepted, after he'd discussed it with his wife, a lawyer, who agreed with the provost's position *vis-à-vis* the fleeting nature of the deal. She'd been helping the local hospital lay-off workers ever since the economic downturn had begun and knew whereof she spoke. After thirty-five years at Magnolia University, in the same office—on what had jokingly been referred to as the Unproductive Wing, at least until being unproductive had become more of a liability than usual—he was out of a job, left with nothing but his lifetime library privileges. The day after he submitted final grades, he submitted his keys, as well, and drove his possessions home in his pick-up truck. He would have felt sick, depressed even, if he weren't still walking around in a daze.

The truth was that Dunbar had no clear plan for his retirement. He'd daydreamed about spending his Golden Years puttering around his English garden, but three decades of work had left nothing for him to do. He'd replaced the scraggily, clover-infested fields with Bermudagrass, planted Groundsel, American Beautyberry, and Bigleaf Gallberry bushes, and lined the perimeter of his eight acres with stately White Oaks, saving more colorful Tulip Trees for the interior. He and his son, from his first marriage, had built a pier that jutted out into the pond at the center of the property, and a local sculptor had cast three iron nymphs that sat on concrete pillars in the murky water. His dream garden had been achieved.

Faced with a summer centered around shuttling his daughters from activity to activity, he did what he always did when at a loss: he retreated to his books. Sitting on the floor surrounded by the unpacked boxes from his office, he went in search of inspiration. What better use of his time than the writing of a *magnum opus* that would shame Nickerson for putting him out to pasture? At the end of an afternoon, however, he had nothing but sore buttocks to show for his work. It had been seven years since he'd completed *Off With His Head: Pride's Purge and the Rump Parliament*, about Charles I's execution, and many more since his lone success: *The Protection of Capital in English Law, 1720-1800.* The thought of embarking on a project that could easily take him into his seventies seemed too daunting, especially when his wife was hinting about him picking up classes at the local community college. At the bottom of a box of books on the House of Stuart, he found *The Complete Guide to the English Garden*, a fifty-year-old encyclopedia as thick as a metropolitan phonebook. He remembered coming across it in the local bookstore after he'd first moved to Mississippi and the almost physical pain elicited by its sixty-dollar price tag.

Over the next few days, while he mowed the acres of lawn that surrounded his modest home, he thought about the *Guide*, about the excitement he'd once felt, following it step-by-step, creating the closest thing to a classic English garden that he could in such an inhospitable climate. It had been akin to the thrill of watching his three children being born, of experiencing their milestones along with them. But he never got that thrill any more: Jenna, his youngest, was twelve, and her older sister, Kat, fifteen. They didn't seem to need him. And his son, Andy, had a family of his own, in Memphis.

Dunbar's property was divided into quadrants with the pond in the middle. His remodeled home and detached garage comprised one quadrant, as did the separate garage where he kept all of his landscaping tools and machinery. The remaining two, the ones closest to the road, were empty fields that a neighbor woman kept pestering him to hand over to her prairie reclamation project. Sitting atop his riding mower in the upper of the two fields, he suddenly had a vision of something far grander than a habitat returned to nature. He didn't know where it came from, exactly, though he could trace the germ of the idea back to those books in his study, the *Guide* chief among them. When he looked through the swarm of mosquitoes at his well-tended enclosure that afternoon, he pictured the outline of a majestic structure rising above the tree line to the east. George Dunbar was going to build a folly.

Not just any folly. What he saw before him was a replica of the Battle Abbey, in East Sussex. Built by William the Conqueror as penance to God, and Pope Alexander II, for the blood shed during the Norman Invasion in 1066, the Abbey sat on the field where the Battle of Hastings had taken place. William had died before it had been completed, and the centuries had been less than kind to the building, all but destroyed by Henry VIII. It remained as nothing more than a facade, which was exactly what Dunbar's folly would be. He relished the thought of building the faux ruins of an actual ruined abbey. Plus, he remembered a line he'd read in a book once: *Unlike the erection of other ornamental objects, folly building flourished in times of hardship, when their construction served as a form of poor relief, providing work, and therefore wages, for peasants and unemployed artisans.* His wife had a good job, so economic hardship wasn't in their immediate future, but Dunbar still saw himself as someone in need of relief.

*

"What do you think?"

"Mom's not going to like it." Jenna, Dunbar's youngest, stood next to him, hands on her hips, watching the men pour the concrete footing for the folly.

"We've already discussed it. She's fine." Dunbar had wanted to do everything himself, but the time it would have taken to mix and spread the cement, not to mention the danger of fouling up the entire project with one miscalculation, had convinced him to hire a local firm for the crucial first step. When Jenna remained silent, he said, "Why don't you think she'll like it?"

"It's big," she said. "Really big."

Dunbar ran his hand along his brand-new mason's hammer, itching to get started. The first load of bricks—blonde waterstruck, guaranteed to look 200 years old upon delivery—sat on a pallet near the cement truck, useless until the footing set. In the meantime, the project lived on in its ideal state in his mind.

"What's this thing even for," Jenna said. She spun his chalkline in the air like a yo-yo.

"It's not *for* anything. It just *is*. Like the nymphs in the pond."

She snorted. "The skinny dippers?" Before Dunbar could correct her, she corrected herself. "Joke. I don't need a lecture on Greek mythology. The bedtime stories were enough."

Once the men had finished and their truck had rumbled down County Road 319 in a plume of diesel exhaust, Dunbar led his daughter around the perimeter of the structure, pointing out which sides would be built highest, where the bricks would have to be split to look as though they were crumbling. "William the Conqueror ordered that the altar be placed at the exact point where King Harold fell in battle."

"I'd like to renegotiate my fee," Jenna said. "This is going to take way longer than I thought."

Dunbar had offered both of his daughters an hourly wage for their help, but Kat claimed she would be too busy with The LadyKillers, her alt-country band— whatever that was—to help, so he'd been left with only one assistant. In the past, he might have asked his wife to take some vacation time and pitch in, but now that he'd been deemed unnecessary by the university, he was eager to prove his resourcefulness, particularly to the one person whose opinion of him mattered most.

Shortly after the publication of *The Protection of Capital in English Law, 1720-1800,* he'd been invited to give the keynote address at the law school honors society's annual dinner. His future wife had been a third-year student, and the recipient of most of the top awards. She'd impressed him, afterwards, with her questions about the Poor Law and Combination Acts, and had made it clear during several coffee dates that she found him equally impressive. He'd dated sporadically after his first marriage had ended, a too-young match exacerbated by the lack of opportunities for his wife in northern Mississippi, but he had never thought of himself as the type to date someone closer to his son's age than to his own. In the years since, people were often disappointed that Megan hadn't been his student, that nothing scandalous had gone on between them. The age difference was still enough to make Dunbar conscious of his own mortality, to keep him going to the gym, fighting the daily battle with eyebrow-and-nose hair, and regularly updating his wardrobe. Being mistaken for his daughters' grandfather was bad enough. He refused to be seen as his wife's doddering father.

The next morning, younger daughter by his side, he set the mason's line around the perimeter of his folly. His father, a master carpenter, had passed on his love of manual labor to all three of his sons and that love, combined with the two hours he'd spent watching tutorials online, had helped prepare Dunbar for the work ahead. He mixed the mortar in a wheelbarrow, showed Jenna how to transfer it to the mortar board and load a trowel, how to spread it evenly on the bricks, including when to scrape off the excess and when to leave it alone. Jenna was a quick study. Within a half-hour, he was able to leave her alone and concentrate on hauling and setting the first tier of bricks.

By lunch, his hands were already sore, calluses appearing as tiny buds beneath the skin of his finger pads. The bricks were heavier than he'd imagined, and he knew already that he'd underestimated how many it would take to fill each tier. He intended to insert a perpendicular layer of bricks, both for variety and stability, after every three horizontal layers, which would require even more bricks that he hadn't ordered.

The work went slowly but steadily throughout the afternoon. Dunbar stripped down to his undershirt, offering Jenna his pullover to wipe the mortar from her blond hair, but she declined. Every time he complimented her work, she shrugged, then turned away, smiling to herself. When Megan arrived home from the hospital, where she was senior legal counsel, they'd completed an entire course, including the perpendicular row that had frayed Dunbar's patience and used up Jenna's remaining mortar.

"Correct me if I'm wrong," Megan said, shooting her daughter a look, "but this is bigger than we discussed."

The three of them stood in the middle of the folly, where the first rows of the congregation would have sat, centuries earlier, listening to a priest drone on in a language they didn't understand.

"It only *seems* larger, because you can't see the scope of the project yet."

"We never talked about a budget," Megan said.

"I'd rather talk about what a great job Jenna's doing. She's already a pro!" He bent down to point out the details. "We're using an English garden wall bond, with a header after every three stretchers. This means quite a bit of work for Jenna, I can assure you."

"Why do I feel like you're trying to confuse me."

"*Educate* you. Once you know what we're doing, you'll be as excited as we are!"

Jenna looked at her mother, shrugged once more, and headed toward the road leading up to the house. "I need to get cleaned up," she said. "If that's okay, boss."

Once she was out of earshot, Dunbar told his wife, "She tries to hide it, but she was really getting into it."

"Sure she was." Megan gave him what he thought of as one of her courtroom looks, one part impatience to two parts bemusement. "You could use a shower yourself," she said.

✻

They completed the first story by the Fourth of July. The folly was eight feet tall at that point, with the rear side left half complete. Dunbar's t-shirts had grown snug at the shoulders and arms from the muscles he'd developed, and even Jenna's forearms were toned from the repeated scraping and smoothing of the trowel. The American Beautyberry bushes around them had turned from a rosy red to purple, and the summer's heat sent them indoors by mid-afternoon, where they drank sweet tea and laid on the hardwood floor, letting the living room's ceiling fan cool their sweat-soaked bodies.

The morning after the Fourth, Dunbar awoke to find his daughter standing over him. She'd been shaking him for some time, she claimed, but since they'd begun working on the folly, he'd been sleeping more deeply than ever before. Jenna's words threatened to overturn this hard-won peacefulness.

"We've got a problem," she said. "A big one."

Still in his bathrobe, Dunbar followed her outside. The air was sticky, like walking into a warm mist, even though the sun was barely above the tree-line. Jenna was silent, marching purposefully toward the folly. When they were within sight, she pointed at the offending structure and waited for his nearsighted eyes to adjust.

"What happened?" he said. The upper half had collapsed on two sides, bricks strewn all over the ground. Some sections looked as though they were still deciding whether or not to come down: the lower courses twisted, mortar bulging out of gaps that shouldn't exist, the upper ones leaning at precarious angles.

"All this work gone to waste," Jenna said.

He didn't know what to say. He wanted to go back to bed, get up in an hour and see if this wasn't all just a bad dream.

"You ever hear of a buttress?" Jenna waived her smartphone at him and continued. "Five minutes online and I know all about them. Shit, Dad. What were you thinking?"

"Language," he said, but he knew his chiding lacked authority. She was right. He'd been kidding himself thinking that he knew what he was doing. What if it had come loose while Jenna had been standing beneath it?

He picked up a fallen brick, ran a fingernail along the jagged mortar. "I guess it'll be more of a ruin than I thought."

"What?"

"I'll pay up once I go to the bank. Then you'll have the rest of the summer to yourself."

"You're *quitting*?" She looked angry, threatening, shaking her trowel at him.

"I'm afraid we've exhausted my limited expertise," he said.

"If we can build eight feet up from the ground, we can build a couple of buttresses. They're just fat walls."

"But what if something else goes wrong? I don't want you getting hurt. Besides, once your mother finds out—"

"Who says she has to know? We'll tell her we noticed a flaw or something. That we had to rebuild."

As much as the ease with which his daughter crafted a believable lie bothered him, Dunbar was bolstered by her enthusiasm. He had a tendency to "go negative," as Kat would say. That attitude had killed too many projects to count while they were still in their infancy. He'd abandoned manuscripts after years of research simply because the first draft didn't come together as smoothly as he had dreamed they would. He owned a piano, guitar, and harmonica that he'd tried, briefly, to learn. And he still cringed at his one attempt at local theater.

"We have to do something before your mother leaves for work. She'll see it from the road."

Jenna smiled. "I found some tarps in the garage. Should we add a Closed for Remodeling sign?"

It took three weeks for them to rebuild the walls and add the necessary supports. Dunbar was as embarrassed by his failure to notice the buttresses on the original Battle Abbey as he was proud of Jenna for asserting herself. She calculated how wide and tall the supports needed to be, how many bricks they would contain, and how far apart they should be. In the end, they added two to the front and three to each side.

The completion of these improvements also marked the upper limit of his agreed-upon budget, so Dunbar took one morning off in late July to meet with the Dean of Instruction at the local community college. He wore a linen suit with a white shirt and red-and-blue striped tie and mistook the Dean, in Polo shirt and gray trousers, for a student waiting for an audience with what he assumed would be a more professionally-attired, and significantly older, administrator.

"We're pretty relaxed around here," Dean Zelinski said. "You can call me Curtis."

Curtis Zelinski? The name sounded a bell deep in his brain. But before he could place it, Zelinski said, "My brother, Chris, was one of your students. From what he told me last night, this meeting is certainly pro-forma. If you won't mind my saying so, Magnolia's loss is our gain."

Dunbar nodded. Not wanting to let the entire day go to waste, he'd shown Jenna how to use a mashing hammer and blocking chisel so that she could split a stack of closure bricks they'd need to make the folly look authentically decayed. Instead of listening to Zelinski, he wondered how she was doing, worried that the task was beyond her and that she'd give up or, worse, do a lousy job.

"...afraid the most I can offer you at this time is a Western Civ survey," the Dean said. "We're mostly American-centric here and don't have much need for British history."

Dunbar swallowed his objections, grown rote over the years. How can you understand American history, his protest usually went, without knowing the history of the country it sprang from? The country, the Empire, that was one of the world's greatest powers for four centuries? Instead, he resigned himself to the slight and said, "Western Civ One or Two?"

Curtis's mouth twisted to one side and he fidgeted in his chair, doing his best imitation of a beginning actor's portrayal of discomfort. "We've condensed our curriculum somewhat in recent years, eliminated excessive requirements in order to help students make quicker progress. Studies show, especially at the two-year-college level, that students are more likely to drop out if they feel that the course load is unnecessarily onerous."

"Which means..."

"We've combined the two Western Civs into one. Which should be a boon for you. The students are more engaged because they aren't beaten down by required classes, and you have the freedom to choose whatever you want to teach from the entire sweep of Western history, so long as it's in the approved textbook."

Dunbar left the meeting thoroughly demoralized. He hadn't taught Western Civ since graduate school, but even he knew this was no way to do it. How was he supposed to cover the Stone Age through 9/11 in fifteen weeks? Preposterous. Almost as preposterous as the high school-level textbook Dean Zelinski had handed him on his way out, which contained more illustrations, photographs, and flowcharts than it did actual text. In its fifth edition, the book allotted more pages for Acknowledgements than it did for the Napoleonic Wars. Dunbar had rarely used textbooks in his classes, preferring primary documents, even in undergraduate surveys, where he at least expected students to gain familiarity with the *Magna Carta*, the 1628 Petition of Right and 1689 Bill of Rights, and a smattering of Edmund Burke, not simply a collection of historical sound bytes in overpriced form.

At home, he pulled the car onto the grass and marched toward his daughter. She was still splitting bricks, the finished ones littered around her in pieces as though she'd tossed them over her shoulder when she was finished with them. As he walked, he thought about that smug, juvenile Dean and his admin speak—contact hours, student-centered experience, knowledge-for-transfer—designed to hide the truth, that this job catered to the lowest common denominator, demanding the least amount of fuss from all involved parties.

Jenna dropped the hammer when she saw him coming and fixed her messy ponytail. "How'd it go?" she said.

He waved her off, picked up the mashing hammer. The handle was slick with his daughter's sweat. She'd made more headway than he'd expected.

He split brick after brick, energized by the thought of that ridiculous textbook and the "recommended" syllabus the Dean had handed him on his way out. So much for academic freedom. So much for having the leeway to teach what he wanted. So much for forty years of schooling, studying, and professing.

"Take it easy, old man. You're going to stroke out." When he continued to ignore her, doubling his efforts instead, she said, "Seriously, Dad. Let's take a break."

But he kept going, waving off his daughter's assurance that they had enough bricks. This was his project. He'd know when they had enough. Even though his arms were aching, he kept going, splitting two, three, four more bricks, continuing even after he started to lose his grip, even after he split his left pinky almost in half. Blood poured forth more rapidly than the sweat streaming down his face, more blood than he'd ever seen, even at his children's births, even when his son had broken his leg in a high school baseball game, but he kept going until he became woozy, until his daughter tackled him and threw the hammer into the Beautybushes.

"What the hell's wrong with you?"

"Find my finger," he said, examining the clean cut, right above the top knuckle. He wanted to wipe the blood away to admire it even more closely but feared infection. He was in shock. He knew this, intellectually, even though he couldn't grasp what it meant. That there would be consequences: namely, pain, sharp, nausea-inducing pain.

*

"Have you considered calling it quits?" his wife said. She sat behind him on the bed, rubbing his shoulders. Even this gesture sent lightning strikes through his pinky, already throbbing from the stitches. Vicodin was overrated.

"I can't believe I did that in front of our daughter."

"You could leave the bricks on the ground, like rubble. It might look even more authentic that way."

"She was a trooper, didn't even blink when she picked up the finger."

"You're not young anymore, George. You need to start acting your age."

"What does that mean?" He looked at his finger, wrapped in so much gauze and tape that it was almost as big as the other four combined, which seemed odd, considering it was a joint shorter than the rest. The doctor had chosen not to reattach it, claiming that since the lost half-digit wouldn't impede the functioning of the hand, it wasn't a priority, especially considering his age. What did *that* have to do with it, he'd asked, only to have the question dismissed by the forty-year-old surgeon. "Are you a concert pianist?" he'd said, "or a court stenographer? If not, I don't see where giving you back fifty percent the range of motion you used to have is worth the hassle of the surgery." Spoken to anyone else, he would have admired the man's bluntness.

"I'm not going to lecture you, especially right now." Megan shifted on the bed so that they were face-to-face. "But is that any way for a sixty-four-year-old man to behave? I never should have agreed to this project."

"I don't need your permission," he said. Stitches and Vicodin. He'd lost half a finger and that's all they'd had to offer? Six weeks in a splint, showering with a plastic bag over his hand to keep the wound dry, six weeks he wouldn't be able to work on his folly.

"You see yourself as some lord of the manor," his wife said. "But look at you. Can you even tie your shoes?"

"I'll be fine," he said.

And he was, thanks to Jenna, who soldiered on without him. She laid and mortared bricks, made lunch, and, yes, tied his shoes for him. She was his lifeline—not Megan, who continued to look on with disapproval— until she began school in mid-August, at which point he commenced ripping apart the syllabus Curtis Zelinski had given him and building it back up from scratch. His first day free of the stitches, splint, and gauze, he spent the morning on the scaffolding, mortaring bricks, and the afternoon preparing for his introductory class at the community college.

That night, he stood before his students, all thirty-eight of them, with his chisel and hammer poised above the instructor's copy of *The Bradshaw Survey of Western*

Civilization. "In this class," he said, "we will read the most important documents in Western history, unfiltered by the views of publishers who see their textbook divisions as ever-increasing cash cows." With that, he brought the hammer down, splitting the book in half and burying the chisel in the desktop. The students jumped at the noise. While he worked the blade out of the wood, he added, "Everything we read is in the public domain, so I don't care where you get it or if you read it in hard copy, on your computer, or on your phone, *so long as you read it.*"

When he asked for questions at the end of class, a young man held up his copy of the *Bradshaw* and said, "Will the bookstore take this back?"

Dunbar shrugged. "I'd recommend pulping it." By the next class meeting, one-third of his students had dropped the course. He didn't care. Twenty-five was a more manageable number.

Throughout August and September, they compared the floods in Genesis and *The Epic of Gilgamesh*, read a carefully curated smattering of Plato and Aristotle and the bloodier portions of Sophocles, Homer, and Virgil, and studied the epistolary styles of Seneca, St. Paul, and St. Augustine. Each week, Dunbar provided his students with the best that had been thought and written in the Western world, augmented by whatever knowledge he'd gleaned over the years, and each week, more students fell by the wayside. By the time they moved to *Beowulf* and the Anglo-Saxons, Dunbar had only eleven students.

"Don't be boring." That's what both of his daughters said when he asked for their advice.

"Your standards are too high," his wife said. "Just because it's a required class doesn't mean it can't be a little bit fun."

His wife would have gotten along with Dean Zelinski. After several emails expressing his concern at the falling enrollment, the Dean called Dunbar into his office. "I'm concerned about your enrollment," he said. "It keeps falling."

"When you hired me, you said sixteen was the average class size. With that in mind, I'm merely slightly below average."

"We expect a certain amount of attrition, but you've lost more than seventy-percent of your students. In an entry-level course. That's never happened."

"There used to be a belief that not everyone was cut-out for college," Dunbar said. "That's considered elitist now, I know, but that doesn't mean I can't hold my students to some minimal standard." He hadn't expected to make a speech, had planned on letting Zelinski do most of the talking so that he could get out of the office as quickly as possible, but once he got on a roll, as his family and remaining eleven students knew, he couldn't be stopped. "If this course is going to transfer to Magnolia, or any other four-year school, the students should have to meet the same expectations. If they can't do this in an entry-level course, what point is there in having them hang around for another semester or three? The term 'weed-out' class has too many negative connotations for my taste, but why shouldn't they be challenged? If it were me, I'd want to know if I was cut out for this. If I am, great. If I'm not, I'll save my money and move on to Plan B."

Zelinski looked like he'd just witnessed a high-speed, ten-car pile-up. But instead of twisted steel and severed limbs, he was face-to-face with the educational philosophy of George Dunbar, PhD. If he were an Anglo-Saxon warrior, he'd have a nickname like Dunbar the Great Reducer. He'd vanquish tribes of Inclusionists and Low-Standard-Bearers. Instead, he was an adjunct at a community college in northern Mississippi, where he was defeated by a Dean who had pledged allegiance to The Bottom Line. "I always expect some growing pains with new hires," Zelinski said. "Especially those who come from four-year schools. So I don't want to overreact here. However, if you lose any more students, we're not going to be able to continue this partnership."

Dunbar cancelled class that night and went home to his folly.

From the top of the second story, nearly complete, he looked out on what he'd done, not just recently but over the thirty-five years he'd lived there. He'd been unable to afford anything larger than a quarter-acre in the university town, so he'd convinced his first wife to move to out into the country, where they'd have privacy and all the space necessary for the brood of children they'd planned on having. But to his wife, privacy had felt like isolation, and the brood of happy, outdoorsy children they'd planned on stopped with Andy on account of a difficult delivery. No matter how Dunbar had shaped the land, he'd been unable to make Colleen see that living there wasn't so bad. Finally, when Andy was four, she'd moved him back into town, to a condo she paid for with her job as a copy editor for university publications. She'd never forgiven him for taking her away from her family and her beloved Ithaca.

Alone, he'd funneled even more of his energies into the property. He'd had the pond cleaned and stocked, added Groundsel bushes, with their billowy white flowers and penchant for attracting butterflies, all around the perimeter and made sure the Galberry Holly, White Oaks, and Tulip Trees all stayed trimmed. He composted and studied natural remedies for the various pests and climate challenges of the Deep South. Later, he rebuilt the pier overlooking the pond so that it could hold more people, then began inviting colleagues to his house when he discovered that he didn't have enough friends to fill the new space. He'd wooed Megan with lavish meals served on that pier, by candlelight, the flames dancing up and down the bodies of the water nymphs in the pond.

Balanced carefully on the top of the folly, he realized that his work was nearly complete, that he had almost nothing left to do. Wind blew through the oaks, and he let himself sway back and forth with the breeze even though giving up control frightened him. He waited until the rustling in the trees had died away to climb back down to the ground.

✳

Two days later, he stood before his students, explaining the migratory pattern of the people who became the Anglo-Saxons when he had another, even sadder, realization. Not one of the eleven was paying attention. He looked around the room, wondering who would be the next to drop. Would it be Tyten, the HVAC repairman, who hoped a degree would get him a job as a bookkeeper? Would it be Gloria, who worked in a nail salon and just wanted to know enough to keep up with her children's homework? Or perhaps it would be Holly, a recent Haywood High graduate who'd managed to learn absolutely nothing about subject-verb agreement or any major historical event in twelve years of schooling. Ultimately, it didn't matter who it was. Someone would be next, like the plot of a bad Agatha Christie novel. He didn't care about getting fired by Dean Zelinski—at least not *that* much, he didn't—but he took it personally that he'd been unable to reach them. He had a wall full of teaching awards, he felt like telling them. That should count for something.

"Anyone know what a folly is?" he said, leaving the origin of the Jutes for another time.

"A mistake?" Brie Foster said. Like Holly, she was a Haywood High product, though unlike her classmate, she was only there to save money on required courses.

"That's one definition," he said, then explained the project he'd spent the past four months working on. "This weekend, I intend to lay the final brick. And seeing how the Battle of Hastings is relevant to what we'll be discussing next week, I think it would be educational for you all to be there."

He heard groans from all over the room. At least at Magnolia the students had made some attempt to stifle such a reaction. "Complain all you want," he said. "But there will be food and drinks. And music."

"Is this required?" Tyten said.

"I don't think it can be," someone else said. "It's not during class time."

"Tell you what, if you come to my house, eat my food, imbibe my drink, and watch me put one final brick in a sixteen-foot-tall monument to western civilization, I'll increase everyone's grade by one letter."

He erased the map of Europe he'd drawn on the board and replaced it with detailed directions to his house. Suddenly everyone, even Tyten and Holly, had folly fever.

Everyone but his older daughter. "I don't know why you need a band just to show off that dumb thing you wasted the summer building," Kat said.

He thought he'd been subtle when introducing the subject of The LadyKillers playing what he'd come to think of as a party, not merely an extra-curricular event. But Kat had always been good at sniffing out obligation, so he added, "I'll pay."

She put down her phone and looked up. "How much?" she said.

"Forty bucks per person, not to mention the priceless educational opportunity."

"Lay off the *educational* stuff and we'll do it. I'll have Mandy send you our rider."

"Your what?"

"Our requirements. You know, catering, accommodations, and other stuff."

"You're fifteen. You don't get *accommodations.*"

"Then *you* don't get a band."

So he wasted Friday morning, when he could have been finishing the folly, wandering the aisles of the local grocery store looking for Boar's Head Double Gloucester Cheddar Cheese, Wellington Organic Flax Seed and Wheat crackers, and assorted flavors of bottled teas. Once he'd iced down the tea, per Mandy's request, he picked up Jenna at the middle school so the two of them could attack what was left of the folly. While Jenna chipped away at the edges of the bricks that would make up the top level, providing the distressed look Dunbar desired, he laid and mortared the rest like a man possessed. He *was* possessed. By the thought of his students, his daughters, and his wife marveling at the finished product. Kat would see that what he'd spent all these months on wasn't *dumb*, Jenna would have the satisfaction of being part of something larger than herself, and his wife would realize that all the money they'd invested in the folly had been well spent, that it wasn't mere ornamentation. It was a 320 square-foot stand against mediocrity, in all its Nickersonian and Zelinskian forms. As for his students, he simply hoped that it would keep them interested enough to finish out the semester.

If he couldn't keep them in the room, he couldn't teach them anything.

In his exuberance, he looked down from the scaffold at his daughter, who'd earned a not inconsiderable fortune as his assistant, and said, "This has been fun, hasn't it?"

She blinked away a cloud of clay dust and rested her hammer on her shoulder. "It hasn't been that bad," she admitted, then went back to smashing bricks.

✳

Dunbar lit the torches half an hour before his students were to arrive, aiming for the most dramatic effect possible. He'd affixed sconces to the interior and exterior walls that morning, even though it ran contrary to the original Battle Abbey's construction, positioning them to ensure that no part of the structure would be left in darkness. By the time the last of his students had arrived, he had burgers and hot dogs going on two grills and The LadyKillers were set-up on the pier. It had been Kat's idea to put the band down there, illuminated by another quartet of torches. The music came to him on the wind, like a dream, and he was relieved that they sounded more alt than country, though he still had no idea what that meant.

Megan worked the buffet table, passing out buns and condiments, fries and onion rings, and doing her best to keep the three minors in his class away from the beer, while Jenna offered tours of the folly, unprompted. In a gap between songs, he heard her tell Holly and Brie, "I did a little bit of everything. Mortaring, laying brick, squaring the corners. It's not that hard, actually, if you work at it." He hoped to hear more, but The LadyKillers launched into their signature song, "Can't Spell Killer Without Her," before Jenna could continue.

Once everyone had eaten but before they had a chance to get tipsy, Dunbar led the group around to the back of the folly, where he'd ringed the scaffolding with white Christmas lights and aimed a spotlight at the corner where the final brick would be laid. He climbed quickly, noticing that his little finger no longer hurt when he grasped the metal rungs, and signaled for the band to stop playing. Unnecessarily, it turned out, as the band's four members had already abandoned their instruments and begun walking toward him. From the top of the scaffold, he looked at the strange group below. His wife and Jenna, Kat and her friends, all eleven of his students, ranging in age from nineteen to mid-fifties, looked up at him, even Tyten, who'd eaten three hot dogs and a hamburger, washing each one down with a beer, and Holly, who called his construction a foully.

He did his best to savor the moment, but now that it had come, he wanted to lay the brick as quickly as possible, tear down the scaffolding, and challenge Tyten to a beer-drinking contest. His first wife would have accused him of being in *one of his moods*. Broody, she'd called him. But that wasn't it, not exactly. He'd hoped that turning the completion into an event would stave off the feeling of futility he got at the end of a long project. But even this party couldn't keep him from fearing that all he'd done was build an elaborate variation on the garden gnomes and lawn jockeys his mother had favored. What if he hadn't proven anything beyond asserting his own hubris? Whoever owned the property next would tear it down, he was sure, or worse, turn it into a children's playhouse. It would never last, not the way he wanted it to. He hadn't built a monument; he'd erected an encumbrance.

Before he could banish such thoughts, the sound of a single voice drifted up toward him. He couldn't make it out at first, not in his distracted state, but once he began paying attention, he heard the word "folly," repeated, rhythmically, over-and-over again. Someone was chanting. He squinted and searched the faces beneath him until he found the chant's origin. Tyten. He had a beer—his fifth? —raised aloft in Dunbar's direction while he urged on the assemblage with his free hand. Soon others joined in, Jenna and Megan chief among them. By the time his entire class had picked up the chant, even Kat and The LadyKillers were shouting as well. He didn't care if she would later claim she was being ironic or sarcastic or whatever else she was always being, it felt good hearing her cheer for him.

He waved to Jenna, encouraged her to join him, but she wouldn't, yelled something he couldn't hear above the sixteen other voices raised in unison. "Folly—folly—folly," they shouted. The LadyKillers' drummer kept time with her drumsticks, hitting a rung of the scaffolding so hard Dunbar could feel it all the way at the top. He studied each face, trying to commit their expressions to memory. He knew that some of them, his students, members of the band, would laugh about this

60

moment later, but after he set the final brick, Dunbar couldn't resist raising his arms in triumph.

GOOD INTENTIONS

It's not a cult, he told himself. It's an *intentional community*. This had become his mantra during the three-hour drive south to visit Cassidy, his daughter. She'd called that week, for only the third time since her wedding, and he'd been so glad to hear from her that he'd agreed to everything. Of course I'll bring all of your old children's books, he'd told her, and even though one-quarter of the drive was unpaved, he'd be glad to make the trip on one of his rare free Saturdays to check all the children's teeth. And he wouldn't dream of expecting payment.

With the trunk full of moldering boxes of Eric Carle, Beverly Cleary, and Roald Dahl, and a large tackle box of dental supplies rattling in the backseat, he and his wife, Cassidy's stepmother, bumped down the gravel road leading to the compound.

"You're muttering," Pam said. "And they don't call it that."

"That's what it is."

"Cassie says it's an intentional community."

That term again. What the hell did it even mean? Was this place really anymore *intentional* than their neighborhood in St. Paul? They'd spent five weeks looking for the right spot, another two negotiating with the seller. Wasn't that intentional? But he knew better than to ask. Even Pam was on board with what she referred to as Cassidy's *lifestyle*.

Pam's willingness to make the best of things irked him sometimes, the same way it bothered him that she called his daughter Cassie, which neither he nor Cassidy's late mother had. Even Pam's outfit—hiking boots, flannel-lined khakis, sweater, and wind breaker, she always dressed in layers—got on his nerves. While she had the perfect ensemble for every occasion, he'd scrutinized his third of their closet for twenty minutes trying to determine what one wore on one's first visit to a cult. In the end he gave up and stuck with the jeans and sweatshirt he'd had on in the first place.

The road was washed out in spots, so he had to pull onto the scrub, risking the car's paint job and side mirror every time he dodged a hole and careened toward the trees. Branches snapped beneath the tires, reminding him of the time, only weeks after she'd gotten her license, when Cassidy had almost broken an axle on his Audi; somehow, a three-foot tree limb had gotten jammed in one of the front wheel wells, though she denied having anything to do with it. The trees, almost bare, flew by to either side while he looked straight ahead, studying the road's dips and inclines, the pools of rain water and smatterings of leaves.

"Slow down. I saw kids running around up ahead."

Once he eased off the gas pedal enough that they weren't being thrown back and forth against their seatbelts, he, too, noticed a couple of little ones running in the field to the right. They had long sticks in their hands, the smallest boy straining to keep a dead tree limb upright, like a jouster.

"It's *Lord of the Flies* out here."

"They're having fun. Didn't you ever play in the woods?"

"In the city? We played street hockey and tried not to get run down by Mrs. Applewhite's Buick."

They came around a sharp bend and arrived in a clearing so abruptly that he had to use both feet on the brake to stop in time. They skidded to a halt in front of a semicircle of low buildings, all evenly spaced. A half-stripped minivan sat on blocks to the right and various paths connected the huts, led off into the trees, and disappeared. People descended on them before he could take the key out of the ignition, kids pressing their dirty noses and dirtier hands to the window, their mothers unable to pull them back. Reinforcements trickled out of buildings that looked like the hooches he'd searched in Vietnam.

"I feel like we're on a *National Geographic* expedition."

"You promised you'd be on good behavior."

"I'm purging myself of impure comments."

The children backed up long enough for them to get out before coming even closer, touching his jacket sleeves, hands, belt-buckle. Even though they'd driven south the whole way, his breath still showed in the cold air, and the earth crunched beneath his feet. When he opened the trunk, the kids scurried over, arranging themselves in a row with their arms out.

He heard a voice, knew within the first two syllables that it was his daughter's. "I told them about the books. They want to help you unload."

He looked up and saw her at the front of the car. She looked good. Her cheeks were pink, her blond hair longer, held back in a pony tail. She had her mother's slender frame, and the blue wool sweater that hung from it covered her hands and billowed down to her hips. Before he could get to her, Pam wrapped her arms around her. The two embraced, forming a closed circle.

"Are you?" Pam said.

She nodded, smiling as her eyes teared up.

"How long?"

"How long what?" he said.

She pulled her sweater tight against her now-bulging stomach, and the children danced around her.

Pregnant. It all made sense now. Her call, the books and dental supplies, all an elaborate ruse to get him out there. She was stubborn, like him, wouldn't want to admit over the phone that she'd been wrong to quit her job and shack up with a cult leader. At least she had finally seen the light. But it also meant that a child was on the way, that he would soon be a grandfather. He'd have to start a college fund. First, they'd need to clear out the guest room. And Cassidy couldn't possibly get a job until after the baby was born, so he'd need to see about health insurance. So much to think about.

But instead of sharing any of this, all he could get out was, "I can't believe you're pregnant."

"Five months."

The children slowed him down, but he waded through them as best he could, reached for his daughter, who gave him a gentle hug, pulling away too quickly for him to get a proper grip. Pam slid her arm through Cassidy's, and the pair walked toward the closest hut, leaving him to stumble after them with his supplies. He'd definitely packed too much, though from the looks of these urchins, he had a busy day ahead of him.

His only child was pregnant. He was going to be a grandfather. But instead of celebrating such news and planning his daughter's return to civilization, he found himself on a Doctors Without Borders mission without crossing any borders. Inside the hut, the unfinished floorboards were shiny from wear, and a brown handmade rug, messy with fringe, lay in the center of the room. A matching runner led from the doorway to a reclining lawn chair next to a low wooden stool. Above, thick beams supported the gray tin roof. A slender chimney cut through its peak and descended into a small wood-burning stove across the room that a woman was tending to.

"Do you have electricity? I can't clean teeth without power."

"We have a generator," she said.

For the next three hours, he saw child after child, between two and eleven in age. None of them squirmed, and though they all had dirty faces and grubby hands, when they opened their mouths he saw clean, unblemished teeth. Not one trouble spot. But whenever he asked them questions intended to put them at ease—favorite TV shows, school subjects, Vikings or Packers, the same ones he asked all of his young patients—they either stared at him or spoke gibberish. They were too old to be behaving this way. He imagined widespread learning disabilities, malnutrition that had stunted the language acquisition centers in the brain, a made-up dialect designed to confuse law enforcement during the inevitable stand-off to come. Most of all, he feared that his granddaughter—he'd already decided on the sex—would have the same problem, that he wouldn't be able to communicate with her.

He and Cassidy used to talk all the time, holding long conversations even in her difficult teen years. Because of her mother's ALS, Cassidy had relied on him for rides to basketball and track practice, and in those years, he had discovered the magical properties of motion. As long as the car was in gear and he looked straight ahead, she would go on and on, telling him about school, of course, but also the boys she was interested in or those interested in her, what she wanted to do after college—Teach for America, an NGO in Africa, take a year off to hike the Appalachian Trail, he remembered them all. He had to grip the wheel to keep from reaching out and grasping her hand in his euphoria, which he knew would ruin everything. Now, she shared those moments with Pam, if they happened at all.

After he'd seen the eighth child, an older boy with a wicked overbite, his son-in-law, Ray Thielen, entered. In his late-thirties, he had a beard that would have made Walt Whitman feel inadequate.

"Everything all right, Dr. Prenshaw?" Ray had never called him by his first name.

"That last one has quite a malocclusion—"

"I meant the drive. You found us okay?" Ray dropped into the lawn chair. Would he want his teeth cleaned, too?

"Oh, sure. It only took two sets of directions, GPS, and a map. If you want a free GPS, I tossed ours out the window on 61, around Winona."

His son-in-law smiled, yellow-stained teeth appearing in the middle of his beard. "Always trust the map. That other stuff is too smart for its own good."

"I didn't really chuck the GPS."

"I used to be an engineer, remember. I know all about how those things work. That's why I'm telling you—*trust the map*." He ran a hand through his beard, hard, sending black, brown, and white flakes into the air between them. "Now, about those teeth?"

"You want me to check yours?"

"I meant the kids, doc. How are they?"

"That last one will need braces in a few years."

"Why do we view every imperfection as a problem? Seems to me that crooked teeth are more desirable than going years with metal bonded to them."

"You're the one who asked. He's got a hell of an overbite, which could cause problems beyond getting a date to the prom."

Ray folded his arms across his barrel chest. Everything about him was as oversized as his beard—his hands, chest, feet, ego. He'd worked for Boeing before moving to Minnesota and going off-the-grid, as he called it.

"Tooth decay, pressure on the TMJ. These aren't cosmetic issues."

"Any other problems?"

He wished for a litany of ailments that would impugn Ray, the leader of this group, but the children's teeth were healthier than the ones he saw in his office. "They could use more folic acid in their diet," he said, though this was true of almost everyone.

"I'll take care of it."

Ray had used that same line over and over the first time Gary met him, at Cassidy's apartment in Stillwater, where she'd moved after college. Even though she was working in a fancy French restaurant, Ray did the cooking—braised lamb, roasted new potatoes, fennel salad—and hopped up from the table constantly to *take care of* whatever needed taking care of. He had the beard already, but it was trimmed and well-groomed.

Cassidy had shared little about Ray with Pam, even less with him, so much of the evening consisted of the typical Getting to Know You questions, the sort he'd become adept at after years of grilling Cassidy's boyfriends to ensure that they weren't deadbeats or budding sociopaths. She'd gone through boyfriends quickly, not because she was overly-demanding, he'd decided, but because she jumped into each relationship so impulsively that they moved through to their natural conclusions even faster than usual. Just when he'd gotten the name of one boyfriend down—particularly difficult when Cassidy was in her Jason-Joshua-Jackson phase— they would break up and she'd be on to the next on. For this reason, he didn't pay much attention to Ray, beyond noting that at least this one could cook. It bothered him, a little, that he was twelve years older than Cassidy, but he liked that Ray had a decent job—designing wind turbines for an alternative energy start-up—unlike Cassidy, who'd parlayed a $160,000 liberal-arts degree into a waitressing job, even if it was one that required her to say things like *Tome d'Aquitaine* or *turbinado blancmange*.

But after dessert—Cassidy's contribution, her mother's apple filbert tart—as the wine flowed more freely, Ray grew expansive, first about the evils of corporate America—a popular topic—and later about travel. "I'm so glad I went to Afghanistan before Bush fucked it up," he said. "A buddy and I hiked the southern Silk Road from China to Merv, in Turkmenistan, after we quit at Boeing. We wanted to keep going, but crossing into Iran—no thanks. Don't get me wrong," he said, as though any of them knew their geography enough to question him on this, "we cheated at times—we weren't about to climb K2—but we did some of the lower peaks in the Karakoram and the Hindu Kush. So much of it's ruined now. I wonder if anyone will ever get to do that

70

trip safely again." He poured the last of the Malbec into his glass, then sat back and stared at the ceiling.

"I think the Soviets and the mujahideen had something to do with the damage," Gary said.

Ray blew air from between his lips. "Not on the scale of the U.S. military. You know how many tons of bombs we dropped?" He finished his wine. "I don't want to make this political. All I'm saying is that that was an amazing fucking trip. You do much traveling, Dr. Prenshaw?"

"I once spent thirteen lovely months in Southeast Asia."

Both Cassidy and Pam gave him a look, but he ignored them.

"I've been to the Philippines and Malaysia. Beautiful beaches."

"Dad was in Vietnam," Cassidy said, her face reddening.

Ray nodded, saluted Gary with his empty glass. "I get it. I talk too much sometimes."

"It's okay, baby," she said. Turning to Gary and Pam, she added, "He's nervous."

"You know, when the sniper fire stopped and the smoke cleared, it almost felt like a vacation. Then someone would yell *Corpsman*, and I'd try to patch together a shoulder or wrap a pulpy stump that used to be a foot."

Pam had him out the door within ten minutes, wouldn't talk to him until the next morning. Cassidy gave him the silent treatment for two weeks. He and Ray never mentioned that night again.

For this reason, they'd never discussed her decision to leave her job and move into the woods. He only found out when she called from a nearby gas station, talking so fast in her excitement he had trouble keeping up. Great new opportunity. Live our values. Escape materialistic American culture. He held his tongue this time, only mentioning that he'd be there if she needed him. "This isn't a fad," she said. "This is a new beginning." That was the end of that.

After a lunch of lentil-and-vegetable stew, he and Pam finally had some alone time with Cassidy, who led them on a tour of the environs. They left the communal dining hall, passed the open-air kitchen, where the women were cleaning up, and picked their way past the children, eagerly dumping scraps onto a sprawling compost heap. Cassidy pointed to a cluster of shacks fifty yards away that held the wood and metal shops, the smoke- and slaughterhouses, and the dairy, all but the last the province of men.

"Ray and Gregg—did you meet him? —did an amazing iron trellis for a house in Red Wing. It had ivy weaved into the support beams and the family's coat-of-arms at the top. As they were pulling away, the next door neighbor came running down the street waving a blank check, so they made one for her, too."

"I'd like to see that," Pam said. "Sounds beautiful."

"Ray has their addresses. You could stop by on your way back."

She described the trees they passed, the White Ash and Sugar Maples, and their uses. Gary couldn't believe the ease with which she did this, how casually she'd bend down, pick up a leaf, and explain the differences in length, texture, something she called lobes. She even knew the shapes and sizes of their seeds. "Ray wants us to learn how to make syrup from the Sugar Maples. We'll use it as a sweetener to cut back on cane sugar."

The trees opened into a clearing, where cows roamed in the field before them, a few pigs penned to the left and half a dozen goats to the right. It was so quiet he could hear the grass tearing from the earth as the cows grazed. He'd never been so close to the creatures, who looked imposing behind a skimpy barb-wire fence.

"They aren't nearly as big as industrial farm cows," Cassidy said, "because we don't stuff them full of grain and keep them trapped in one place."

Pam walked up to the fence. "Is it safe to touch them?" Before Cassidy could answer, Pam had reached out and begun brushing the neck of the nearest one. The cow lowed at first, then seemed to lean into her hand like a house cat would.

"I hate goats," Gary said. "When I was—"

"*When you were a boy* one butted you to the ground and tried to stomp you at Aunt Jean's."

"Sorry to repeat myself."

"Lighten up. Aunt Jean tells it differently, though. She says *you* taunted the goat."

73

"I'd never been out of the city before. As soon as we pulled up, they all came running. I thought they were going to charge. When I realized it was a game, I thought I'd play along. Guess we had different rules."

"That's why our child is going to know how to fend for herself." He tried, and failed, to hide his reaction. "I know you don't approve—"

"You're *staying* here?"

"Why wouldn't I?"

"It's just—I thought—" Gary looked at Pam, leaning over the fence to reach the cow even as it backed away. He could have sworn he'd read this situation correctly, that by the end of the day he'd have worked out a plan to get Cassidy back to civilization.

"Oh, Dad. You didn't think I was coming with you."

"Not exactly," he lied, the truth being too embarrassing. "But what happens when your baby grows up, wants to go to college or get a job? She'll have no idea how the real world works."

"This isn't the 'real world'?"

"No jobs, no benefits, certainly no savings. Do you even pay taxes?"

"Ray says your world is what you make it, and I agree. We're happy. Our baby will be, too."

Pam turned around, brushing dirt from her hands. "I can't believe how calm they are. So affectionate." She wrinkled her nose. "What's going on?"

"Nothing," he said.

"That's right," Cassidy added. "First, I found out Dad came here to save me from this evil, brainwashing cabal. Then he said I'll be mistreating my baby if he or she can't go to McDonalds and spend twelve years filling in bubbles on standardized tests."

"I didn't say any of that." He looked to Pam for support, but no matter what he did, he couldn't get her attention. She was focused on Cassidy.

Two of the older boys came out of the trees behind them, a gray mutt crashing through the undergrowth at their heels. They walked a wide circuit around the cows, counting aloud as they pointed to each one, before moving on to the goat pen, where one of the creatures came up to the fence and allowed itself to be stroked before galloping back to the others.

He hadn't said anything about *saving* Cassidy, about her *mistreating* her child. That didn't mean such thoughts hadn't occurred to him, but what father, in his place, wouldn't have reacted the same way? True, it seemed bucolic, livestock tame enough to pet, growing all one's own food, but what happened when someone became ill? What if, God forbid, something happened to the baby?

"Have you at least seen a doctor?" he said.

"Tara's a nurse, and a doula. Don't look at me like that. She's delivered our last three babies, all without complications."

"Your mother spent thirty-two hours in labor with you."

"I'll be fine."

"Of course you will."

A cow bellowed, and he looked up in time to see two calves gamboling in the pasture. They were using an older one—the noisy one—as an obstacle in what looked like a game of tag.

"We should head back."

"Yes," he said. "We don't want *Ray* to worry."

"That's why you haven't been here sooner," she said. "*Ray* actually pushed for this visit, not me. I told him you'd be an asshole, but he insisted."

Pam grabbed his arm hard enough that he could feel her fingers through his sweatshirt and jacket. "They're both adults. It isn't your place—"

"Easy for you to say. She isn't your daughter."

She let go. "Would you like me to wait in the car? Or should I start walking home?"

"Pam—" Too late. She'd already begun trudging down the path.

"Way to go, Dad. You want to try pissing off the cows next?"

He watched his wife's receding figure, noticed that even though she was watching her steps carefully, she still seemed unsteady, as she did whenever she wore high heels. Halfway down the hill she lost her balance, one foot slipping against the damp earth; she waved both arms in the air, struggling to stay upright, then settled back into her normal gate. She was no more comfortable out there than he was, so why couldn't he make an effort, too?

"I'm sorry," he said. When Cassidy didn't respond, he remained silent, trying to figure out what to say that would limit the damage. "What do you expect when I never see you, can't even call you, and then you spring this on me?"

"See her?" Cassidy pointed toward Pam, almost out of sight. "Be more like her."

"If your mother were here..."

"Don't bring her into this."

He waited until his wife had disappeared into the trees. "You can't pick and choose your family when it suits you."

They retraced their steps, the crunch of dead leaves and frosted earth their only accompaniment. He knew he was right. When Lori had gotten sick, Cassidy had pulled away, never touched her mother, had to be guilted into spending time with her, but towards the end, when her mother had become bedridden, Cassidy sat next to her, weeping more tears than he'd thought humanly possible. She yelled at the nurses and doctors, the hospice workers, and him, her sixteen-year-old indignation even more strident than his private grief.

She behaved the same way in college, not returning phone calls for weeks at a time, until he threatened to fly to North Carolina and camp out in front of her dorm room. Then she'd come home for breaks, rent his favorite movies even though she'd seen them countless times, didn't even like some of them. She would stay up late, falling asleep next to him on the couch, where they'd awaken in the morning, curled against each other.

He paused in front of the carpentry shop, listened to the wheeze of a saw going through a board. The door was ajar, and though his daughter kept going, he pushed it open with his toe and walked in, waiting for Ray to stop before announcing himself.

"You need something, Dr. Prenshaw?"

"Just a safe haven."

"She can be prickly. I think it's hormonal," he said, smiling. "But I'll never tell her that."

"That's impressive." He ran his hand along the board. Bottom to top, no splinters or rough patches. "Mahogany?"

"Maple. But once I stain it, you won't know the difference."

"Truthfully, I pissed off my wife as well."

"Some knack you've got. Remind me not to pick it up from you."

"Don't worry. I was born with it. Hopefully the child won't get it." He frowned. "You're going to *stain* it. What about all the chemicals?"

Ray snorted, put down his saw and picked up a plane that looked older than either of them. "Even I make compromises."

"Greatest good for the greatest number?"

"Sort of. Our generator's starting to go."

"Uneasy lies the head..."

Ray laughed deeply this time. "I'm no king, but I can sympathize with old Henry there." He ran the plane along the board several more times, sending up a puff of sawdust. "What, you didn't expect me to know Shakespeare?"

"Aeronautical engineering, farming, woodworking. A regular Renaissance man."

"I prefer the Enlightenment. Hand me that jig, will you? This is getting dull."

Gary walked to the bench, examined the rows of tools, a mix of the well-worn, like the plane, and the pristine—screwdrivers with tips so sharp they looked like they'd never bit into metal, hammers with unsullied grips. All of them in neat rows. He picked up one of a series of jigs lying off to the side. "Quite a collection."

"My father's. The other men contributed as well."

"My grandfather was a weekend carpenter. I spent my youth holding boards, sweeping sawdust, and playing gofer while he made bookcases and picnic tables."

Ray clamped the plane blade into the jig, sharpened it against a water stone.

Gary opened one of the work bench drawers. He waited until his son-in-law had finished and said, "This cordless drill is expensive. I've got a smaller version at my office."

"Dental tools are specialized. Cost more." He handed Gary the jig.

"The children get used books and you get new tools."

"No reason to buy new when old books will do."

79

"Spoken by the man surrounded by a thousand dollars' worth of tools."

"You see a lock on that door? Anyone's free to come in." He looked up at Gary, then said, "Keep pushing this and you can add me to your pissed-off list."

They stepped closer to each other, almost instinctively, until they were within a few inches. Gary's pulse quickened. He hadn't been in a fight in decades, figured he didn't stand a chance against his son-in-law, several inches taller and broader than him, but that wouldn't keep him from trying. He could smell the lentil stew on Ray's breath, see the crow's feet around his eyes, the way his flared nostrils disappeared, at the corners, into his mustache. Gary made fists with his hands, remembered what his father had taught him: go for the nose. No one wants to fight back when he feels like his face has been flattened.

Ray shrugged, stepped back. "The real truth? Will, Curtis, and I drove to St. Cloud and liberated some of these from Home Depot."

"You *stole* them?"

"Ever notice where most of that stuff is made? China. We sit back while this behemoth—that's trying to dominate the world, economically, the same way the U.S. and its allies have militarily—takes advantage of us and pays their own workers shit. And we're so complacent we ignore the 'Made in China' stickers and the huge markups these megastores add to products designed to break within a year so that we have to keep going back to buy replacements. They're no better than drug dealers. Poisoning us to feed their own avarice."

"I thought people like you went after Walmart."

"I'd love to, but they treat shoplifters—their word, not mine—worse than casinos treat card counters. Besides, none of the big box stores are innocent."

"My daughter knows about this?"

"Everyone knows." Ray took another step back and reached behind him for something on the bench.

"You're going to get caught."

"I'll deal with that if it happens."

"And my daughter?"

"Will be fine. She's resourceful. Now, I need to finish this while the light is good."

Gary walked back toward the huts, passing through the trees whose names he'd already forgotten, almost knocking over a rain barrel when he came around the corner. Children chattered in the clearing while their mothers prepared dinner in the communal kitchen. He lingered outside the open-air building, watched them stir pots suspended over open flames, chop vegetables and leafy herbs, slice the fat off a ham hock. He wondered if the cast-iron skillet his daughter now carried toward the fire had been *liberated* like Ray's tools, and if she'd helped to do so. His daughter a thief? The more he tried to understand this place, the more confused he felt.

He continued on, into Cassidy's hut, where he found Pam, alone, flipping through a picture book. She didn't even look up, suddenly engrossed in *Where the Wild Things Are.*

"You have every right to be mad at me. But can you save it until we get home. I could use your support right now."

She licked her finger, turned another page.

"I've messed up this whole day." He went down on his knees before her, desperate. He'd prostrate himself if need be. The book fell to the floor when he grabbed both of her hands. "Ray and the other men have been *shoplifting* supplies. And the women—Cassidy—don't care."

"That's nothing."

"Nothing?" With Ray, he'd felt like a detective interrogating a cagy suspect, but now that he had scored a hard-earned confession, the D.A. was uninterested.

"I was talking to one of them—Molly, I think—and I asked her about the children, about what language they're speaking, and she told me... You need to talk to Cassie."

"Why'd you stop?"

"Because there's a reason the phrase 'Don't shoot the messenger' has been around so long."

Back at the kitchen, he found Cassidy sitting on the stool he'd used that morning, shelling peas into a child's bucket with large, faded daisies on it. "Have a nice visit with Ray?" Her fingers separated peas from their pods with metronomic precision.

"Is it sanitary to prepare food like this, out in the open?"

She kept shelling in response. "You can't help yourself, can you? Pick, pick, pick."

"I hear you have another surprise for us."

She scooped up more peas, dropped them in the folds of her sweater. Please God, he prayed, let Pam have been overreacting. He didn't think he could handle any more revelations.

"Something about languages. Ray just filled me in about China's plot. Don't tell me he wants you to learn Chinese in advance of the revolution." He wanted his voice to sound light, carefree, but couldn't hide his anxiety.

She finished the peas and led him away from the others. Her fingers were cold against his wrist, almost to the point of stinging. He hadn't felt her touch since he'd led her down the aisle. She'd been married outdoors, at a state park, with fewer than thirty in attendance. Only later did Gary learn that Ray had refused to secure a permit, that they could have been fined for the ceremony.

"I don't know who told Pam—I'm sure Ray won't be happy—but we're all learning Frisian. The kids just pick it up faster."

"Frisian?"

"Technically, West Frisian. As in Friesland, a province of the Netherlands."

She offered this explanation as though such details were foremost in everyone's mind. He was so tired of the aggressive posturing that he felt like saying, Of course. I read the *Friesland Post-Gazette* every morning with my Gouda on rye. Instead, he tried to be diplomatic. "Don't they speak Dutch?"

"Frisian is more authentic. Ray's ancestors, and his parents, speak it. So do most of the inhabitants."

"I don't understand."

"Think about it."

He didn't want to say it, had to force himself to get the words out. "You're *moving* there?"

"This was a trial run while Ray worked out the logistics. He's a dual-citizen, since his parents are Dutch. The climate is similar, there's plenty of arable land, and they have a long history of supporting alternative communities."

"Ever hear of Jonestown?" He ignored her glare and said, "When were you going to tell me?"

"I thought the pregnancy was enough for one visit. Don't worry, the baby will be born here. Ray says we won't be ready to leave for at least six months."

"This doesn't make sense. None of it." He dropped into a catcher's squat, joints cracking. He'd worked hard all his life—college, the military, dental school, his practice. He'd loved his wife, Cassidy's mother, taken a four-month leave from work at the end, loved his daughter even more fiercely after Lori's death. Even refused to date Pam until Cassidy, a college senior at the time, gave her blessing. He'd done everything right, hadn't complained when he'd been drafted a month after marrying Lori, hadn't blamed God or the universe when she was taken from him, hadn't stood in the way when his only child wanted to marry a man so much older than her with ridiculous ideas about wealth redistribution and intentional living.

"How did I fail?" he said.

She smiled, at last, crouched down next to him, and took his hand, hers warmer now. She rested her head on his shoulder, burrowing into the nape of his neck. He wrapped his arm around her, felt the curve of her pregnant stomach with his fingertips, palm resting on her ribcage. When she'd been born, her ribs had heaved with her gasping, sputtering breaths. She'd been premature, impossibly small, and he'd tried to hold her almost without touching her, he was so afraid of crushing her delicate body. Now, he gripped her side as hard as he could, even when they almost toppled over. The firmness of her pregnant stomach surprised him, as Lori's had. In some way he couldn't pinpoint, this tactile sensation made that moment, his daughter's life, the life growing inside her, real to him. Sentimental as it was, he wished the baby would kick just then, let him know everything would be all right, but it was too early for that. Cassidy had been active all the time, not just somersaults and kicks but what Lori called playing the piano with her toes. Myra Hess, she called her.

His wrist began to cramp, and he let go. But before Cassidy could stand up, he said, "Is it difficult to learn, Frisian?"

"A lot of dialects. But the alphabet is basically the same as ours." She smiled again, the first full one he'd seen, one big enough to show off all the dental work he'd done over the years. "You thinking of learning?"

"If the mountain won't come to Mohammed..."

Pam appeared before them, his dental kit at her side. "We should go," she said, "if we want to make the highway before dark."

He loaded the car, fiddling with his equipment to forestall saying goodbye. It still didn't make sense. The day had gone so quickly. He had so many more questions. When he closed the back door, Pam reminded him of the digital camera in the glove box.

"You're not opposed to photos, are you?" he said to his daughter and her husband. "They don't steal your spirit?" When he saw their matching looks, he added, "A joke."

The two couples stood together, in front of the huts, while one of the older children took several shots. After each one, Gary called, "One more," and held his daughter tightly.

Finally, they got in the car and waved to everyone—Cassidy and Ray, the other adults, the filthy, polite children with gleaming teeth and a strange new language—before bumping back down the access road. The camera sat between them in one of the car's beverage holders.

His mind spun faster than his tires in the muddy ruts. He wanted to look at the photographs, double-check that they were in focus, that Cassidy had been smiling as broadly as he remembered, but every time he reached for the camera, another jagged rock appeared in their path, or they arrived at an unexpected hairpin turn. He had to be patient. Sooner or later, they'd reach the predictability of the blacktop that would lead them back to civilization, and home.

SHADOWBOXING

I learned of my sister's death from the internet. Like so much of what was written about her, the post made up for a lack of facts with innuendo and attitude:

TROUBLED PAINTER SARA FRYE FOUND DEAD EARLIER TODAY. Unconfirmed reports imply she died at own hand. Might the art world's '*enfant terrible*' have saved her most *terrible* for last? Regardless, it's the end of a once-promising career. She was 35.

I hadn't spoken to her in two weeks, which wasn't unusual, and I didn't hear from her husband, Ravi, for several more hours. She had killed herself, he told me when he finally bothered to call. She'd done it in her studio, in Pennsylvania, with a gun neither of us had known she possessed. When he finished, I began to thank him for finding time to call me himself, but he cut me off. "Don't make this about you, Anita. You don't get to have some special claim on her. Not this time." But he was wrong. I'd been through too much with her for it to be otherwise.

I remember when she got her first camera, a Polaroid. She took it everywhere. To school and to church, on Girl Scout outings and to the movies, where she'd sit up front and take photos of the unsuspecting audience, momentarily blinding them and getting herself banned from two Dallas multiplexes. She loved the *shucking* sound the machine made as it spat out each print, reveled in the brief moments before the image materialized. She often made a series of attempts, laying them side-by-side and scrutinizing the differences—the changes in the light and the way this affected the texture and color, how different angles made it possible to de-familiarize the familiar, highlight ordinary aspects of the unusual.

She was a change-of-life baby, born sixteen years after our parents had given up hope and adopted me. The gap meant that while she was mastering her camera, I was weaning my first child. When my husband and I arrived home for Christmas that year, baby in tow, I was disappointed that she didn't come out to greet us. She usually bounced up and down, so excited to see her nephew that she'd make smacking sounds with her lips until I handed him to her. But this time I had to seek her out. She didn't answer when I knocked on her bedroom door, though I could hear muttering from within, so I called her name.

"Auntie?" She had often mixed up the sounds in my name as a toddler. Auntie had been the one to stick. She turned the lock and opened the door. "I'm so glad you're here." Everything was dramatic with her, ordinary phrases imbued with a breathless intensity that alarmed strangers.

Three of her bedroom walls were covered, floor to ceiling, with Polaroids. "Thumb tacks won't work," she said, "so I use nails."

"How does Mother feel about this?"

"She made me promise not to hit my thumb." She rolled her eyes. "Like I'd do that on purpose. That's why they call them *accidents!*"

A coffee can filled with nails sat on her desk next to a hammer that looked too big for her to lift. She'd been born prematurely, so tiny that when Daddy first saw her, he told the doctor, "Put her back in. She's not done yet." Even full grown, she would be an inch under five feet and as sturdy as a street sign in a hurricane.

I studied the Polaroids, moving from wall to wall as though I were in a museum. No, more like a photographic hot house. It felt claustrophobic. Unless I focused on a specific image—a perfectly formed boot print in the mud, a defaced bus shelter ad for a needle-exchange program—my head started to spin.

"Doesn't this give you a headache?"

"Dr. Ware gave me pills."

"What kind?"

"Yellow ones."

"What are the pills *for?*"

"Look at these. They're my new favorites."

In a row on the wall next to her bed were three photos of her hair popping out of the top of a turtleneck, like flowers in a vase. The pictures had been taken in an angled mirror, each one coming a little closer to centering the image.

"Your hair's green."

"And blue and orange."

She flashed her familiar grin.

"No way Mother let you do that."

"I used markers. Did it while they were in Galveston."

"They left you alone?"

"Grammy Jeanette—" her godmother, giver of the camera and anything else she desired— "stayed with me. I washed it out before they got back."

"I think I like the off-center ones best."

"That's what Jeanette said. 'Off-center pictures for an off-kilter girl.'" She giggled and flopped onto the bed.

When I asked Mother about this later, while doing the dishes, she said they found it easier to give in. "She's been spunky since she was born. Why else would she want to come out so early?" She continued before I could respond. "Jeanette has more energy to keep up with her." I had to remind myself that Mother was almost sixty, Daddy two years older, and that their Miracle Baby was more than most young parents could have handled.

As casually as I could, I said, "Something seems off, don't you think?"

"Dr. Ware says she has Attention Deficit Hyperactivity Disorder." She said this slowly, as though the words alone had the power to conjure up more problems.

"Have you seen her room? Her attention seems fine to me."

"I'm just telling you what he said. Jeanette's making an appointment with a specialist. We'll get to the bottom of it." With that, Mother closed the door on the discussion. I knew better than to broach the subject with her again.

*

Like the rest of us, Sara went to A&M, where she majored in Art Education, a compromise with our parents, who found a studio degree too impractical. She even pledged the sorority that Mother and I had joined. She had a boyfriend, an Omega-Pi she brought home for Thanksgiving, where he played football with my eldest, feigned interest in the younger one's LEGO constructions, put up with Daddy's jokes about being The Interloper. All in all a good sort, though a little bland. which is why it seemed so strange the following spring when the school blamed their break-up for Sara's suicide attempt.

Daddy had recently had knee-replacement surgery, and because Mother had to stay with him, I made the ninety-minute drive from Houston to College Station to find out what had happened. By the time I arrived, no one who'd been on duty when Sara came into the ER was there, so I waited for the university's Crisis Liaison, as the title on his business card read, to arrive.

"She's fine now," he said. "They stitched her up and sedated her for the night. She said she hadn't been sleeping, which probably contributed—"

"She tried to kill herself because she was *tired?*"

"No one's saying she meant to kill herself. A suicidal gesture, most likely."

"She slashed both wrists."

"In a dormitory bathroom stall. She wanted someone to find her."

He paused to study me. I considered saying, You've never seen a Korean before? Heard of international adoption? Instead, I held my tongue and waited for him to continue.

"Our understanding is that your sister has become withdrawn. When she and her boyfriend broke up, she needed a way to make others notice her."

"She's in a sorority. How is that withdrawn?"

"She hasn't been to a meeting or function since January, and she's been missing most of her classes for almost as long."

"And no one thought to look into this until now?"

"Her RA talked to her about becoming more involved, offered to help her find a student organization to join. She wasn't interested."

"After all this you think she made this *gesture* over a broken heart?"

"You teach high school. You know how emotional girls—all teens—can be."

On campus, her RA let me into her room, whistling at what we found. The room remained dark even after I flipped the light switch, and the smell of patchouli made my sinuses tingle. I stumbled toward the windows and reached for the curtains. They came off the rod when I pulled them, but still no light. Sara had covered the windows in tinfoil, covered that with trash bags, and tried to seal the curtains with masking tape. These layers came away one at a time, slowly illuminating the disaster area that was her room. She'd even put black tape over the tiny lights on her cordless phone charger and the smoke detector, and turned her alarm clock, my graduation gift to her, to the wall. Dust particles hung in the air like ash after a volcanic eruption.

Her RA pointed down and said, "She'll have to pay for that."

She'd tiled the entire floor in a mosaic of black, gray, and blue, each one-inch square. A swirl of black threatened to envelop the blue like a massive wave, the gray outlining the places where the process was in mid-act.

"No wonder she hasn't been going to class."

"You didn't find any of this worth reporting?" I said.

"I haven't been in here since Alison moved out in February. But, you know, Sara's not exactly normal."

"It's like you people want us to sue you."

She backpedaled toward the door, reached behind her for the knob. "I don't know anything about that. You'll have to talk to the Hall Director."

I walked around the room. Sara had painted the mirror and sink fixtures a flat black. She'd used rubber cement to affix charcoal-colored sheets to the white cinderblock walls. Even the electrical outlets had been covered. She'd draped a sheet over the computer. As hard as I searched, I couldn't find the phone receiver.

Back at the hospital, she flapped her bandaged arms at me and called me Auntie, as though nothing unusual had transpired. Dark circles ringed her eyes like bruises, and her normally pale skin looked translucent. She'd lost weight: her collarbones and sternum stood out beneath her gown. Her blond hair, shoulder-length when she'd colored it with markers years earlier, had been hacked into a lopsided bowl cut that called attention to her pointy ears.

"What did you do to your room?"

"Isn't it great! Jeanette gave me her credit card for the supplies." The words ran together in her enthusiasm. "It took me two weeks. I might tile over it. There's this de Kooning in my art history book. Maybe I should do something original. What do you think about—"

"And the rest of the room?"

"They tied me to the bed last night." She gave me that grin again, the one that would lead a French critic to dub her the *elfen terrible*. "But the drugs...they were *good*. I haven't slept like that—"

"Is that why you did that to your windows, because you couldn't sleep? You weren't blocking out transmissions from Neptune or anything?"

"Do you think I can have more of those pills? Just the square one. The others, the capsules, are made with gelatin. That comes from animal skin."

"I've been up all night. Can't you say something that makes sense?"

"Poor Auntie." She patted my hand. "Do you want to lie down? I can make room."

"Who cut your hair?" I held the jagged ends between my fingers. They were already splitting. "You did it yourself, didn't you? Did you at least use a mirror?"

"I can fix all of it, maybe not the floor, but I think it's *pretty*. They could charge extra for it. Maybe they'll pay me to do all the rooms. I'll be rich!"

I knew then what I had to do, though it took several days to complete the paperwork, officially withdraw her from school and pack up her room. Justin and Henry, my two oldest, agreed to share a room so that I had somewhere to put their kooky aunt, and Joel, my husband, knew enough to keep his views to himself.

Sara stayed with us through the summer and fall, volunteering during arts-and-crafts hour at a nearby nursing home. All of us, even three-year-old Cooper, looked after her. She put on weight, started sleeping through the night, and even tapered off most of the drugs. At Thanksgiving, which we hosted for the first time, Jeanette announced that she'd gotten her into Sarah Lawrence, her own alma mater. She would start in January.

"Wonderful," Mother said. "That's what she needs, to stay busy." We'd all taken to discussing Sara as if she weren't present.

"She's busy here," I said. "I was going to enroll her at the community college. If that works out, she can transfer to the U of H and still live with us."

Joel and Daddy exchanged a look, but Jeanette jumped in before I could say anything.

"Houston's lovely, dear, but it's no place for an *artist*. Sarah Lawrence is the kind of place where she can blossom. And it's so close to the city."

"I know."

Sara and Cooper were making faces at each other, Sara flipping her eyelids inside out, snarling, while Cooper tried and failed to touch his nose with his tongue, as she could.

"What do you think, Daddy?" I said.

"Maybe Jeanette's right. Texas might not be big enough for your sister."

✽

Though it took her five and one-half years to graduate, Sarah Lawrence turned out much as Jeanette predicted. Sara won awards in every category at the student art exhibitions and was even invited to be part of a group show in New York, after which Joel and I moved her into a closet-sized apartment in Brooklyn, while Jeanette helped her get a job at the Public Library and paid for studio space a few blocks away, in an old furniture store.

She lasted six weeks at the library before quitting to become a lackey for Arnaud Duval, the video artist. From her phone calls, it sounded like she and the other assistants were the real artists, the Frenchman simply the front man who attended gallery and film openings and appeared in the *Post* and the *Daily News*. But Sara seemed happy.

One of her tasks was to find actors for Duval's work, and that's how she met Ravi. A fellow artist, he went from a walk-on role in one email to moving into Sara's place three weeks later to being married in another month's time. She brought him to Dallas soon after, both of them sporting matching gold bands, when we gathered for Mother's seventieth birthday.

"When did this happen?" I said once we'd been introduced.

"We wanted to tell you in person."

"*She* asked me," he said, the two of them laughing like idiots. "Three days later we were in front of a Justice of the Peace."

"Christ," Daddy said, "you two ever hear of a church wedding?"

"Watch your language," Mother said, propriety keeping her from engaging in what was really going on.

Even once Mother and Daddy accepted the way they'd gotten married, other complications arose. Just because they had adopted a Korean baby didn't mean they were the sort to absorb an African-American son-in-law into the family without the occasional rough patch. For the rest of their lives, they couldn't understand that Ravi's stuffy, conservative suits were an artist's affectation, not a sign that he was a member of the Nation of Islam. And, not being from the South, Ravi took offense when Mother naively asked, "Where are your people from?"

Jeanette was so thrilled by what she called the Romance of Like Minds that she convinced Sarah Lawrence to host a joint show for them. My sister almost managed to mess that up too. Instead of the urbanals— urban pastorals—she'd promised, her work arrived courtesy of an eighteen-wheeler and consisted of a series of eight-foot-tall replicas of famous dolls and stuffed animals, complete with anatomically correct, and often aroused, genitalia. Her enthusiasm for these creations was such that, in showing them to the gallery curator and the art department chairwoman, she thrust the top half of her body into Raggedy Ann's vagina.

The students loved the show, the school paper devoting all but one paragraph to Sara's pornographic creations. This did not keep the administration from shutting it down three days early on account of complaints from the community. The accompanying furor reached the city, where Sara's answering machine was filled with offers from galleries. She recreated the show in Manhattan but refused to sell to anyone but museums. She wanted her work to remain public, not in the hands of a small coterie of wealthy admirers. This, even though she'd never been in a position to sell anything before. It worked. They sold to the MOMA and the Walker, in Minneapolis, which bought both Raggedy Ann and Randy Andy, and to other museums in Cleveland and San Francisco. In her mind, however, none of these successes topped the excitement of the original show. As the years passed, the Sarah Lawrence opening grew to Woodstock proportions in the art world's imagination; more people claimed to have been there than lived in Bronxville altogether.

*

For a while, all was quiet on the Sara front. Over the next eight years, Daddy got Parkinson's and practically moved into the VA, which led Mother to sell the house in favor of a condo. Justin and Harry graduated from college; and we packed Cooper off to A&M as well. Then Ravi called from New York one July.

Sara had been behaving *erratically*—his word, as though he were a therapist giving an official report—and hadn't been in contact in the nine days since she'd gone to Pennsylvania, where Jeanette had bought them a farm house for an artists' retreat.

"Why didn't you go with her?"

"The show in Montreal took something out of her. I need you to talk to her. We've been having… issues."

"What sort of issues?"

One benefit of getting older, I've learned, is that you're allowed to be nosy. It's as though younger people naturally assume you're interested in their lives, now that your own is practically over.

"A misunderstanding, that's all."

"Is this about a woman?"

"You know I wouldn't cheat."

I waited for him to explain.

"I'm not even sure, honestly. She was so upset when she left, she didn't make any sense. You have to talk to her. You're the only one she listens to when she gets like this."

When I arrived, the house was crowded with people, three different types of music blaring from three different stereos in three different rooms. It looked like a scene from another time: Chateau Marmont in the '60s, or Henry VIII's court at its most decadent. A Senegalese performance artist my sister had introduced me to at least twice stared me up and down without a hint of recognition, then forgot about me when the woman to his left passed him an art deco bong. A couple in their twenties sat in the bay window, staring into each other's eyes while their hands, pressed together at the palms and fingertips, worked circles in the air between them. In the kitchen, a waist-high stack of pizza boxes teetered toward the countertop, a dented metal trash can, filled with empty wine bottles, blocked the back door, and bubbles formed and popped on the surface of the gray water in the sink, like a witch's cauldron. The house reeked of pot, body odor, and what smelled like diapers but turned out to be the Morning Meadow scent from the room spray someone had used to try to cover the stench. My sister's groupies had descended like an Old Testament plague.

A glassy-eyed young man in nothing but jeans that hung so low I could see the dragon's wings tattooed on his pelvis came out of the half-bath off the kitchen and flinched when he saw me. "*Konichiwa*," he said.

"I'm not Japanese."

"*An-nyung-ha-se-yo*, then."

"Where's my sister?"

"Who?"

"Sara. The woman who owns this place you've turned into your own—" I almost said *den of iniquity* but stopped myself. I wasn't as hip as my sister and her friends, but that didn't mean I had to sound like Mother.

"Out back," he said, mumbling, as he fled the room.

I kicked the trash can out of the way and opened the back door, the rush of fresh air an immediate improvement, and followed the path to the barn my sister used for a studio. Even from fifty yards away I could hear the music coming from the house.

I pounded on the locked door with my fist, shaking it on its hinges, until my sister yelled, "Go the fuck away."

"It's me."

"Auntie?" A minute later, the deadbolt flipped, and the door opened. Sara was nowhere to be seen.

The door slammed shut after I walked in, the bolt thrown, and I turned around and saw my little sister pressed against it, as though her ninety-pound body might keep others from forcing their way in.

"Auntie, Auntie, Auntie," she sang as she danced around me in oversized hiking boots, touching my wrist, elbow, hair, and face with her tiny, paint-flecked hands. When I reached out to her, she pirouetted away, sang something I couldn't understand, and smiled her manic grin.

"It's so *wonderful* to see you," she said. She beckoned me toward her, and away from the door, with her curled index fingers. She had on a dingy men's undershirt that covered her boney ass, her tiny breasts and pointy nipples showing through the cheap fabric, the V-neck stretched out of shape. A pair of baggy, green boxing shorts swished as she danced. The thick leather bracelets she wore to cover the scars on her wrists stood out against her pale skin.

I followed her past the curtain my husband had helped her put up, years ago, to separate her studio from the rest of the barn. He'd replaced the leaky roof and installed solar panels to make it self-sufficient like she'd wanted. Behind the curtain, sunlight flooded the room from the skylights in the ceiling.

"Who are all those people?"

"Friends," she said. "Friends-of-friends. Friends-of-friends-of-friends. They keep *coming*. Every time the Amtrak arrives a few more appear."

"They've turned it into a frat house."

"Really?"

"You haven't noticed?" I looked around. Dirty dishes sat on the kitchenette counter, a stool in the middle of the room, and her workbench. A mound of pillows and blankets slumped in the hammock tied between two beams in the corner. "When was the last time you left this room?" As soon as I asked, I wanted to take it back. I wanted to call Ravi and tell him I was finished, that she was his wife and that the problem was between them. I wanted to get in my rental car and head to the airport, not look back until I was home, preferably in bed.

"Want to see what I'm working on?" she said, beginning her dance once again.

As a kid, she'd hummed to herself constantly, making up her own melodies, and I wondered if this same music played in her head now, thirty years later.

"Answer my question first."

She fluttered her fingers in front of her. "I threw my assistants out three—no, four days ago. Is that a long time?"

"Do *you* think that's a long time?" I said.

"I think I'm staying here until *those people* are gone."

"That's the first sane thing you've said."

She giggled. "Oh, Auntie. Come see my piece."

Piece. She'd trained me, years ago, to call them this. Even when they weren't mixed-media—another of her terms—when they were strictly paintings, photographs, or sculptures, they were still pieces. Once, Daddy complimented her on a *painting* and she walked away, wouldn't even look at him until I convinced him to apologize. "It's acrylic on canvas," he said, pointing to the card hanging next to it on the gallery wall. "What the hell else should I call it?"

"I'll look at it later," I said. "After we talk."

She tried to pull me by the hand, then pouted when I wouldn't yield. "No fun."

"I'll be fun after we take care of everyone inside."

Now that she'd finally stopped moving, I could study her up close. Her face was puffy, the skin on her neck mottled and rashy, and her pupils had contracted to the size of the mole on her earlobe. She smelled as rank and feral as the inside of an animal shelter.

"When was the last time you bathed?"

She smiled, touched her tongue to her nose.

"How about sleep?"

"A couple of hours on Monday."

This was Wednesday afternoon, almost evening.

*

It took two days, all of the taxis in a tri-county area, and my bullhorn of a mouth to clear the house so that we could get down to work. I began by confiscating all of Sara's drugs, but coming down from her various highs made her incredibly irritable. She was so stubborn about taking the prescription ones—the mood-stabilizers, the anti-depressants, the anti-anxieties, the anti-antis—that I had to check under her tongue to make sure she'd swallowed. To keep her distracted from the headaches and muscle spasms, and her general grumpiness, we cleaned the house, noting what her friends had broken or stolen as we went along.

"Jeanette always hires a cleaning crew from town," she said after I handed her a bucket of soapy water and a sponge. The kitchen and bathrooms had to be scrubbed from floor to ceiling, three of the house's four toilets unclogged.

"This happens often?"

Sara wiped at the wall with the sponge, more water dripping onto the countertop than reached the intended destination.

"Every time I come here," she said, wringing out the sponge. She'd already spilled a quarter of the water on the dirty tile floor. "Ravi clears them out when they get too crazy."

"Some retreat." When this failed to get a response, I added, "Why isn't he here now?"

"I might be on the verge of a breakthrough, and you've got me scrubbing floors."

"You're not ready for floors. You don't do walls properly."

She didn't respond.

"Tell me about your breakthrough."

"I don't talk about work-in-progress," she said, miffed, as though *she* hadn't been the one to bring it up, the one who'd offered me a preview only days earlier. "The sooner I get back, the sooner it will be finished. Then you won't need me to explain."

She was waiting for me to give in, to acknowledge what a lousy job she was doing and tell her I'd finish on my own, but even if I had to redo all her work, I wasn't going to let her off easy. One of her friends had finger-painted with melted cheese and chocolate syrup on the wall opposite the refrigerator, and while I scraped at this with a fingernail, Sara dumped the dirty water in the sink, splashing the counter, floor, both of us.

"Nice friends you have. You'll have to repaint the entire room."

"This is idiotic. *I'll* pay for cleaners."

The cheese came off in long strips, taking a layer of seafoam paint with it, but the chocolate spread out even more, turning what had been a smiley face into a shit-colored meteor.

Sara flipped over the empty bucket and sat down. "You want to talk about why you're here or keep impersonating Mother?"

"I don't know what you mean." I shifted the kitchen chairs out of the way to attack the wine spills on the floor, another of Sara's tile-jobs. Not the de Kooning she'd talked of years earlier but a Jasper Johns that looked like a crime scene after a triple homicide.

"'Where's Ravi?'" she said in a whiny, needling voice. "He called you—of course he did. He always calls you. Tell him to fight his own battles."

"That's rich coming from you."

"Don't you get tired of being an errand girl?"

"Don't *you* get tired of needing a babysitter?"

We were fifty and thirty-five, engaged in the kind of argument sisters should have had as teenagers.

"What did he tell you?"

"He's worried. He hasn't heard from you."

"He knows why."

"A disagreement."

She snorted. "Try theft."

"You didn't care about anything your friends took when they left here."

"Not *that* kind of theft." She shook her head, disappointed. "You'd have to be an artist to understand."

I scrubbed the floor harder even though it made the stains worse. My frustration had to go somewhere, and it felt oddly therapeutic watching stray bits of yellow sponge adhere to the wine, adding texture to the mess.

"Don't be mad," she said, finally, her voice small. She waited for me to look up, but I kept attacking the stain. "Fine."

She left and stomped upstairs. So help me, I thought, if she goes to her room to pout, I really will leave. After a minute of silence, she retraced her steps, thumping down the stairs and back into the kitchen, laptop in her tiny hands.

"You want to know why Ravi isn't here?"

She flipped up the screen and hit the keys so hard the sound echoed against the dingy walls. If she'd worked like that when she was cleaning, we would have finished the room already.

"Put down the damn sponge," she said.

I sat next to her and looked at the screen. "I read that. It was a puff piece."

Ravi had been in the Sunday *Times Magazine* recently for a show at a famous gallery. It had sold out— he didn't share his wife's qualms about private collectors—and led to rumors that he was being considered for a Genius grant.

"Look at the photo." Sara clicked the magnifying glass icon and Ravi took over the screen. He slouched in a straight-backed chair, left leg draped over one of its wooden arms in a pose that couldn't be comfortable. He stared impassively at the camera.

"Do they teach that look in art school?"

"Forget him. See that painting?" She touched the screen, static snapping in the air when she made contact. "It's mine."

"You share a studio. It was in the background."

"I mean the *composition*. I did a whole series on this flyweight boxer—Hector Mireles—but I didn't like them enough to show. Ravi said *he* liked them, told me not to paint over them. This—" she stabbed at the screen again "—is why. The fucker copied my work, just fuzzed out the details so you can't tell what the guy's doing. Inspired by Basquiat, my ass."

"I thought you said you influenced each other. 'Creative osmosis.'" I remembered this from an article in *ARTnews* years earlier, a pretentious dual profile of art's new Power Couple.

"It's not even as good as mine, but everyone's falling all over themselves because of it. *Oh, the lines,* Ravi. *They're so primal,* Ravi, *so masculine.*"

"All that pot's making you paranoid."

"That asshole at *Paint* who raves about him because he's cerebral—like black people can't go to art school—loves this now, too, because it's so *authentic.*"

"Have you talked to him about this?"

"Of course, but he's like you. 'It's all in your head.' When that didn't work, he told me it was a goddamn *homage.* So I slashed every canvas in the studio. I tore them to pieces while he sat on the floor blubbering."

"Doesn't that suggest he's telling the truth?"

"He's such a narcissist he'd show his used Kleenexes if he could figure out what to call them. *Phlegm on Cotton, Number Forty-Seven.* Three thousand dollars."

"Calm down." Her face was red, the vein in the middle of her forehead so prominent it looked like she'd been branded. "Where are these canvases of yours?"

"Fuck you if you don't believe me."

I stood up, gathered my phone and purse and headed for the door. "No one talks to me like that," I said.

"Please sit down."

Her head was on her folded arms, resting on the table, and she watched me out of the corner of her eye, like she had as a kid when she didn't want the adults to think she was paying attention.

"I moved everything to the warehouse before I left. He doesn't even know about it."

"Jeanette bought you a *warehouse?*"

"*I* rent space in one. The studio isn't big enough for storage. And it's a firetrap. Just because I don't want to sell everything doesn't mean I want to lose it. We'll see what he comes up with now that he can't steal from me. A genius? He hasn't done anything original in three years."

The same had been said of her recently, down to the number of years, not that I'd ever mention it.

"So you're leaving him?"

"The more upset I get at Ravi, the more I like those stupid paintings. I hadn't looked at them in years before I moved them, but they're not bad. Just a boxer throwing punches. No bag, no opponent."

A phone rang, a digital chirruping coming from the kitchen cabinets.

"That's mine," she said. "It wouldn't fit in the disposal."

It rang six times, then stopped.

"That was him."

"You can't know that." By the time I finished speaking mine had begun to ring. Ravi.

"I told you," she said before I'd even looked up.

*

I stayed another ten days, long enough to get the house in order and to get Sara back on her meds. She complained that they made her feel worse than the anti-malarial she took when she was in South Africa, but I couldn't leave her in the state I'd found her in. She still wouldn't speak to Ravi, though I convinced her to at least take her other calls, digging the cell phone out of the bread box she'd stuffed it in. We repainted the kitchen together, singing to the old pop songs on her iPod. Finally, the last few days she locked herself in the barn and continued on her project. It's therapeutic, she'd tell me, then call me *Auntie* in her saddest voice if I tried to object.

I was back in Houston in time for summer's final heat wave. Running errands several days later, I heard the public radio host's soothing voice announce the names of the MacArthur recipients. Ravi's was first, and though I knew they were ordered alphabetically, I couldn't help seeing this as a portent. I pulled over and called my sister, but her cell rang and rang. She never used voicemail. *Each of the so-called Genius Grant recipients will be awarded one hundred thousand dollars a year for the next five years.* Once the foundation cut the first check, I figured Ravi would leave his crazy wife, so at least one problem would be resolved.

I tried her number a few more times that day, though I have to admit the situation seemed less grave as the afternoon cooled into evening. By the time Joel brought the steaks and corn in from the grill, I'd forgotten about it for a blissful half hour.

The phone rang while I was finishing the dishes, someone from Pennsylvania—I never got the name or position straight. An accident. Not over the phone. Next flight to Philadelphia. "We need you here in person," she said. "Your sister left your number in case of emergency."

Emergency didn't do it justice. I knew by her tone that Sara had finally succeeded. If she'd been alive, the woman would have stressed this to keep me calm.

Sara and Ravi shared the same management, and late that afternoon, while I couldn't reach Sara, her rep had. She'd discussed some business and mentioned the grant, then hung up. Based on the coroner's report, Sara killed herself within two hours of that call. "It's amazing she could handle such a large-caliber weapon," a detective told me, as though I should be impressed.

She'd done it in her studio, standing in front of her now-finished piece. She'd even taped an X to the floor, like an actor's mark, for optimum effect.

When Mother announced that she wouldn't attend the funeral—not blaming Daddy this time but the cause of death, which she refused to say aloud—I decided to have the ceremony in Houston, hoping to keep it small. No such luck. The Art World arrived *en masse*, as though they'd chartered a 747. But I didn't see anyone who'd been at the farmhouse. Ravi, in all black, kept his sunglasses on the entire time and had such a retinue that I couldn't get near him until he sat down next to me in the front pew of our church. Months later, he'd hint that Sara did it out of jealousy, which is bullshit. He's just unhappy that no matter what he does, her shadow will always be cast over him.

In her eighties, Jeanette still held court, offering sound bytes to any reporter within shouting distance. She had shed weight as she'd gotten older, become nothing but bone and gristle, and after the service I held her elbow to steady her while she spoke to the man from the *LA Times*.

"Sara was so gifted, such a talent"—no one used the word *genius* "—but like so many artists, she was troubled. The line between inspiration and obsession can be very thin."

"Being an artist had nothing to do with it," I said. It took me a moment to compose myself. I hadn't meant to say that aloud, but since I had, the assembled, even Jeanette, expected more. "Everyone wants to make this so much more noble than it is. She..." I tried to imagine her standing there, sticking such a huge gun into her mouth—one of the crime scene people told me the recoil snapped both of her front teeth—but I can't. "It would be just as awful if she was an accountant, or a teacher."

The reporter waited a respectful moment—a decade would have been better—before saying, "What about the rumor that the act was part of her work? I've heard—"

"It wasn't an *act*," I said. "There's no more work."

Sara left everything to me, so after the probate I returned to Pennsylvania and hired three of the men lingering outside Home Depot to crate the painting. Only one of them spoke English, but even he kept his mouth shut, at first, when they came out of the barn only minutes after entering.

"You'll have to find somebody else," he said, without making eye contact. "We're not going to touch that thing."

I stood in the doorway and watched them leave. I thought about Jeanette, the reporter, all the gallery owners who would have been happy to barge into the studio to pour over every brush stroke, every blood splatter, and declare it a masterpiece, or grotesque sensationalism, I didn't know which. I could have charged admission. *Step right up and revel in human misery. For five bucks extra you can take your picture next to a skull fragment.*

The canvas had to be eight by ten feet, large enough that it seemed like an integral part of the building. An exquisitely-detailed painting done in black and blue and gray geometric shapes, like enormous pixels, filled every available inch. The scale was so huge that it took a full minute before I realized what I was looking at. *Off-center pictures for an off-kilter girl.* She'd painted a triptych of those twenty-year-old Polaroid self-portraits, blowing them up to fit the canvas, even though that cut off even more of the image, more of the hair sprouting from the top of her turtleneck. Much of the detail was hidden beneath the gore, the disgusting layer of dried brown gunk that thinned as it moved towards the edges, the skull fragments—smaller than I'd imagined but everywhere— and various other globs and masses in shades too foul to describe. Copies of the Polaroids, blown-up and subdivided into grids, were taped to the wall next to the canvas, and others, without the grids, sat on the stool to my left, beneath a pallet of dried blue, gray, and black paint, still her favorite colors.

I sat down on top of the stains from where Sara had fallen. Fallen. I hadn't thought of that. The floor was concrete, unforgiving, but surely she couldn't have felt anything by the time she hit it. Even if she had, it would have paled in comparison to the pain in what was left of her head. How long had she lain there, her still-warm body cooling, waiting for the police?

What could have pushed her to this point? I still had no idea. For too long, I'd viewed Sara as a problem that needed to be solved. Maybe that attitude had been the real issue. I'd failed her somehow, that's all I could think. Not that Ravi had or our parents or even Jeanette. Me, Auntie.

I took the original Polaroids with me when I left the barn and haven't been back since. They contained traces of dried blood, though if I stare hard enough, I can pretend they aren't there. I keep them in the bottom of my jewelry box, the safest hiding place in a house full of men. My sons want to turn the farmhouse into a vacation spot for their families, a place where we can gather for holidays and reunions, but as long as I have a say, it will sit abandoned. With any luck, it will cave in on itself.

Enough time has passed that everyone thinks I should cheer up, go back to work, count my blessings— all that nonsense. But whenever I look at them, my sons, my husband, I see that painting. Well, not exactly. The final touches are the same, but it's not Sara's face they cover, it's mine.

BACHELORS

It was a speck on the horizon at first, another farmer riding his tractor through the fields. But as he continued toward it, he noticed it wasn't moving. He drove another hundred yards along the flat, cornfield-lined road before the boxy shape solidified into a four-door sedan teetering upside down in a ditch, tires spinning slowly, free from the August-hot asphalt. Three scratches ran the length of the car like claw marks.

Max slowed down as he passed and honked when he noticed someone on the side of the road.

"Need help?"

The man stood up, brushing the sides of his worn gray suit, and picked up the suitcase he'd been sitting on. A once-white handkerchief was pressed to a gash above his forehead, and his nose was swollen, possibly broken. Without a word, he opened the door and fell into the passenger's seat, the smell of sweat and tobacco about him.

"That's an awful cut on your forehead."

The man looked out the window. "Just drive. The sooner I get away from that piece of shit, the better."

"Where to?" Max said.

"Where are you going?"

"West. If I could drop you somewhere—"

"West is fine."

The late afternoon sun shone through the windshield, and Max pulled down the visor before getting back onto the road. No other cars appeared, and they passed the next fifteen minutes in silence.

"My name's Max, by the way."

"Good for you. I'm Billy Burns."

"What happened to your car?"

"Don't worry about that." Billy's weak chin sloped into the flesh of his neck when he spoke. His coarse, gray hair jutted straight out on top of his head, tapering into stubble around his ears and the back of his neck.

"You sure you want to leave it like that?"

"Forget the fucking car." He blew his nose in the blood-soaked handkerchief, leaving red streaks along his sagging cheeks. "What do you do, Max?"

"I teach social studies."

"Like the state capitals?"

"Citizenship. A little American history."

"Everyone should know the state capitals. I still remember mine. Albany, Annapolis, Atlanta... And the postal abbreviations." He rubbed his hand along the dashboard. "How does a social-studies teacher afford a Mercedes?"

"It's not—well, it is now. My uncle just died. He left it to me."

"You gotta have family," Billy said. "Mind if I smoke?"

"Actually, I do. I'm trying to keep the car as clean as Uncle Dean did."

Billy's cigarette fell out of his mouth, dribbled down his pants, and rolled onto the floor. He kicked at it with his shoe, the tobacco flaking out of a tear in the paper. "Cheap bastard. My old man's name was Dean. Maybe we're related. Cousins or something."

"His name was Dean Street."

"Dean Street? The writer?" Max nodded. "I read all his books. *Murder by Moonlight. The Evil Men Do.* He was your uncle?" Billy made eye contact for the first time. "Pull over when you get a chance. This excitement's got my bladder worked up."

*

The summer he turned eight, he stayed with his Uncle Dean in Chicago while his parents tried to work it out. A week after school ended, Max stood in the Harrisburg train station with his mother, his plaid suitcase and a blue duffel next to him. He would've felt grown-up if his mother hadn't hovered over him while they waited. Brush your teeth. Take a bath. Say please and thank you. At home, he'd been sad about leaving, but now he looked forward to three months away from this.

When he stepped off the train in Chicago, he put on his Pirates cap as they'd arranged in advance so Dean would recognize him. He couldn't remember ever seeing his uncle before, and he vaguely expected a gaunt, Sherlock Holmes figure. But Dean looked more like a football player than a world-famous detective, and he felt surrounded when the man stepped in front of him, broad shoulders and enormous stomach blocking his view.

"Hello there, nephew. How was the trip?"

They shook hands, Max's disappearing all the way to the wrist in his uncle's paw. He tried to come up with a grown-up response, something about the weather or the food on the train.

"Fine," he said.

"You're going to have to speak louder than that. I'm not a lip reader."

Uncle Dean lived on the north side, and on the way home he pointed out Lake Michigan and Wrigley Field, but Max was too busy staring at his uncle's thick beard to notice anything else. His father's face was so smooth it shone, and he had trouble getting used to hearing his uncle talk without being able to see where the sound came from.

"There aren't many kids in the neighborhood, but we'll see what we can do about making our own fun." They pulled into the driveway, and his uncle positioned the car at the very edge of the sidewalk, making it impossible, he told Max, for anyone going to the Cubs game to block them in.

✠

Billy walked out of the gas station on springy, pigeon-toed feet, a twelve-pack of beer in one hand and a paper bag in the other. Max closed the gas tank and met him in front of the passenger's door.

"My turn to drive?"

He searched for a tactful way to put it. "I thought you'd want to stay here and look after your car. They've got a towing service."

"I told you to forget that piece of crap. I bought provisions. You want me to drive or what?"

Max shook his head and walked around the front of the car; somehow, he'd picked up a fare. Billy's temper seemed too unpredictable, so instead of pushing the issue, he turned the key and put the car back in Drive.

"Want a beer?" Billy said. "I also got some donuts and chips. *And* napkins. We want to keep Uncle Dean's car neat. Got a little jerky, too, in case you're interested." Billy pulled a handful of individually-wrapped strips of dried meat from each of his faded pockets. "Nothing goes better with beer. Maybe smoked sausage, but I don't guess you've got any on you."

They followed the two-lane highway west into Iowa, passing through more fields, the smacking of Billy's lips the only sound audible above the clacking of the diesel engine. The sun was lower in the sky, almost eye level, and Max gave up on the visor. He squinted into the distance, imaginary pools shimmering then evaporating on the road ahead, and took a swig from the beer Billy offered him. Even with the air conditioning on, moisture made the outside of the can slick, so he wrapped it in one of the napkins Billy had pulled out of the bag.

"You ever read your uncle's books?"

121

"Never grabbed my attention," Max said. "He wasn't the kind of guy who would bug you about it. Never sent them as presents or anything."

"Humble. I like that. My first wife was a fan. I got bored one day, so I picked one up."

"You're married?"

"Been married three times." Billy sat up in his seat, as if proud of his accomplishment. "First one humped every goddamn man who came to the door but never saved anything for me. Hell, I even thought about dressing up like the mailman, just to see if she could tell the difference. Second one said she was saving herself. That's why I married her. She must've been saving herself for somebody else, cause *I* never got any. The less said about the third one, the better. What about you?"

"I was. Not anymore."

"Kind of young for that."

"We got married right after college. Been divorced over a year now."

"Family values." Billy shook his head, satisfied. "That's the problem with this country. I bet even your parents are divorced. Family values."

*

His first morning in Chicago, Max turned the dial around the nine channels his uncle's black-and-white picked up, waiting for him to come out of the study where he was working. The typewriter keys sounded like rounds of machine-gun fire from an old gangster movie, and he wondered how Dean got his gigantic fingers on the right ones so quickly. Sometimes his dad brought reports home when his secretary was sick, but he only used two fingers, and the hum of their electric machine couldn't compare with Dean's pounding.

His mom had arranged for him to join a reading group at the local library every afternoon, and after lunch Dean ushered him into the passenger's seat of the car. They passed three libraries, though, as they wove around local streets. Max held his tongue, half hoping to avoid going at all and half worried he'd be late. His mom was always late.

They turned down a side street, Comiskey Park looming in the background, and coasted up to a three-story brownstone.

"What do you see?"

"It doesn't look like a library." He tried to speak up for his uncle, but he knew his voice sounded small.

"This is more important. What do you see?"

"A house?"

"Go on."

He stared at the house so long its features started to blur together. He wasn't sure what his uncle was looking for, but he took a stab anyway. "The paint on the porch is two different shades?"

"Good," his uncle said, without looking up from the notebook that had appeared in his lap.

"The flower boxes are empty. And there are five mailboxes next to the door." He was starting to get the hang of this. "Why does one house need so many?"

"No questions, just talk."

"It looks like somebody ran over the trash cans. I guess that's why the garbage is all over the yard."

"Good boy. Let's do a few more."

They drove to two other houses and a newsstand. Max described each to his uncle, whose eyes never left his notepad. It was kind of fun, he decided, imagining who might live in the houses or wondering why Uncle Dean chose these particular ones. By the time, they pulled into their driveway, it was almost 4:30.

"You tired?"

"No." The adult voice rang out this time, and his uncle put his arm around him, guiding him through the screen door.

*

"You want another beer?"

"I think two's enough for now," Max said.

The moon was high above them, like a streetlight leading the way. The fields weren't as densely-planted as before, but Max still had to shake off the sensation of tunnel vision.

"I can't take it anymore." Billy rolled down the window, the night air rushing in, sending napkins and jerky wrappers swirling around the car. "It's not humane.

Three hours without a smoke? Shit. I didn't go that long in Joliet."

"You were—"

"Don't worry. I'll blow the smoke out the window. Won't even use the ashtray."

"You were in prison? Why? When?"

"You're stuttering, partner. Joliet? No big deal. A thing with a FedEx truck. Did a few years that time. Nothing major."

"FedEx? That's interstate commerce. Isn't that a—"

"Whoa, you sound like my lawyer. It was a misunderstanding. I only got one box off the truck before the kid who drove it showed up. Wasn't even anything good. Toaster ovens." Billy leaned back against the seat, cigarette ash fluttering around the car like confetti, and smiled. "Got out early for good behavior."

The car wove, right tires kicking up a cloud of dust before swinging back onto the pavement.

"Hey, now," Billy said.

"When were you in prison?"

"Paroled ten years ago."

"Have you... I mean, you haven't..."

"You got a speech disorder? My kid brother had a lisp. Sent him to a specialist after school. Fixed him good as new."

"*Billy.*"

"Okay. Nothing since then. Three strikes rule, you know."

"What?"

"I go back again and it's over. Repeat offender statute. You teach social studies." He paused for a few beats before adding, "So now I find other ways to get by."

"What kind—"

Billy turned toward him, cigarette-tip illuminating his face like a candle in a jack-o'-lantern's mouth. "Don't worry about that."

"I think I will take another beer."

"Right on."

It was almost eight, and Max figured he could be home by midnight. What about Billy? A ride was one thing; he wasn't about to open a bed and breakfast. But he knew Billy wouldn't take a hint, and he didn't have the nerve to be blunt. For all he knew, telling the truth could get him beaten up and left on the side of the road.

Billy smoked two more cigarettes, lighting each from the shrinking, unfiltered end of the one before it. Max didn't say anything else; he was too busy trying to see through the fogging windshield. Finally, he turned off the A/C and opened his window, sending more garbage flapping around the car. The breeze cleared the windshield as clouds rolled in above them, obscuring the moon. He noticed lights in the distance, some twinkling, some not, and pressed down the gas pedal.

✳

He spent the next morning on his uncle's porch, describing the neighbors' houses to himself. It was a cool day, wind blowing off the lake, and he could hear the clack-clack of the typewriter keys upstairs. He leaned over the railing, studying the yellow, wood-and-brick house next door, proud of his discovery that the windows made it look like a face, when his uncle called, "Get your coat. We're going out."

They drove south, along the lake, got out of the car near Grant Park, and walked toward the Art Institute.

"What's going on?"

"Shh."

Most of the wooden benches were filled with people eating lunch, and his uncle sat down at the end of the most crowded one. Max couldn't find a seat, so he drifted off, lured by vendors' carts on the corner. Hot dogs and chips. Ice cream. Magazines and cigarettes. He imagined strolling up to one, giving a quick nod, and reaching into his pants for a few crisply-folded bills.

What'll it be, pal?

I'm hungry today. How about two? Extra relish.

He'd flip a quarter to another vendor and pick up a newspaper.

How'd the Cubbies do last night?

Same as always.

It's still early.

Soon his uncle was next to him, a large hand on his shoulder. "You still with me, little guy?"

He nodded.

"How about some lunch?"

"Sure." He stepped forward, trying to copy the nonchalance of his imagination.

"I know somewhere better."

At first, he thought they were going home, but Dean steered them to Wrigley for an afternoon game. The small crowd was bundled in jackets and blankets, protecting themselves from the wind. There were plenty of empty seats—the local schools weren't out yet—so they got a pair right along third base, warmed by the sun at their backs.

Max balanced the peanuts in the crook of his bent arm, hotdog in one hand, and his drink in the other as they came up the walkway. Two men dragged long rakes through the infield, drawing parallel lines through the brown dirt. *First you make a hole*, his mother had taught him. *Then you drop in a seed, just like this. Then, in a few months, they'll grow into pretty flowers.*

He pushed the seat down with his butt and bounced into it, spilling Coke on his windbreaker. Two brown beads quivered on the slick jacket, and he scooped them with his finger, leaving faint circles as reminders. Uncle Dean rested his extra hotdog in the webbing of his glove and smeared relish on the first one before biting off half of it.

Dean pointed out the ivy, just a series of dark lines along the wall this early in the summer, and told him about the outfielder who used to stash balls in it when it was in bloom so he never had to search for one during a game.

By the fourth inning the Phillies had scored four runs, and Max fidgeted in his seat, worried that his first live baseball game would be a blowout. In the fifth, the pitcher fired toward the plate, and the Phillies' batter stretched out for the ball, bat extended, a hollow thunk as the curve ball nicked the wood, sending it high into the air above them. Dean passed him the glove, and he stood up, arm outstretched above him, Dean-sized glove enveloping his hand. The ball hung in the air for a second at the top of its flight before it dropped, laces rotating backwards, tailing toward them.

He raised himself on tiptoes, eyes so intent he could see every stitch of the lacing. Thirty feet. Twenty feet. Ten feet. And then the *thwap* of ball hitting leather. But not the sting. He looked up, the world around him crowding in again: another glove right above his, and a man jumping up and down next to him, ball held aloft.

He sat back down, a sick feeling in his stomach, and Dean wrapped an arm around him, pulling him in. Another foul ball came their way later, but everyone ducked, afraid of the line drive. They left during the eighth inning, game already out of reach, and drove the four blocks home, where Dean took him up to his study.

"Some people go to the ballpark and forget their manners." He opened the bottom file cabinet drawer, the sound of baseballs rolling along metal reminding Max of the hailstorm that had smashed their picture window the previous winter. "Go ahead. A consolation prize."

Max counted fifty-two balls, each with a date and a name on it. He reached in, not looking, and picked one out: Don Kessinger. 8/11/75.

*

"I tried to write a book once."

In the light of the restaurant, Billy's suit looked worse than it smelled. The seams were worn, the sleeves stained to the forearms.

After his confession, Billy studied his hamburger, nose dipping dangerously close to the red toothpick sticking out of the bun.

"What happened?"

"I took one of those prison writing classes. Don't laugh. The guys liked my stories. Guess a whole book was too ambitious."

Max had almost finished his sandwich, the "World Famous" Triple Turkey, while Billy only poked at the fries on his plate. "I thought you were hungry?"

"Don't you want to know what it was about?" Billy said.

The waitress appearing with their check offered a brief stay before he gave in, trying to sound interested.

"It was about two brothers. One of them is in prison and the other one, the straight arrow, has to help him out." Billy chomped on his burger, as if the waitress had threatened to take it away when she came back. "See, he may have been framed, the brother isn't sure. So he's investigating to find out if the brother's telling the truth.

It ends up being kind of a Faustian thing. The brother has to decide how far he'll go to get him out. It always sounds good when I talk about it. I just can't get everything to come together."

A Faustian thing? Who was this guy? He couldn't believe it, but the premise sounded interesting. "How far did you get?"

"About two-hundred pages. Really two-fifty, but the last fifty were shit."

"You made it farther than I could have. Maybe you just need to give it a break."

"You think so?" The ketchup-splattered corners of his mouth turned upward as he waved Max away. "Don't worry about it. I'll pay for this."

He pulled a wad of bills out of his pocket, silver money clip straining to keep them in check, and pried a twenty out of the middle. "I always leave a big tip when I can afford it. Used to be a waiter. Shitty work."

Afford it? It looked like he could afford the meal and the tip, and still have enough left over to buy the entire place.

A gray blanket of clouds fluttered above the parking lot. It was after ten, and the Mercedes was the only car in sight. Max walked to the back and opened the trunk, and Billy lagged behind, peering over the edge.

"What's that?"

"My uncle's stuff."

"Photo albums?"

"Scrap books. He kept one for every baseball season. All his ticket stubs and box scores."

"What's in there?"

Max swept his hand over the lid. Billy opened the box.

"Shit. There must be a hundred in here."

"107. Uncle Dean should be in the Hall of Fame. Foul balls were drawn to him. Even if he wanted to, I don't think he could've avoided them."

"What about that stuff?" Billy pointed at two whiskey boxes in the corner of the trunk.

"That's what I wanted to show you. His notebooks. He named me his executor. I don't know what to do with them. I thought only the Hemingways needed executors."

"That looks like a manuscript," Billy said, pointing to a rubber banded bundle of papers.

"It is."

Billy's face seemed to open up, giving him a childlike glow. "Has anyone else seen it?"

"Just us."

✳

Every Friday night, after the dishes were washed and dried, the bachelors, as Dean had begun calling them, walked next door. Dean carried a zippered pouch full of change, which would normally be twice as full by the end of the poker game, and Max tried not to drop the six-pack of Old Style his uncle let him carry. They squeezed through the hedges separating their backyard from Mr. Parker's, the sound of the radio greeting them as they opened the sliding glass door. Most nights, the radio was tuned to a ball game, alternating between the Cubs and the Sox, but occasionally they listened to a local blues station, in celebration of the recent demise of disco.

Max hoisted the bottles into the refrigerator, lining them up in neat rows like the others, and pulled out a bottle of Coke for himself. He always opened the bottles outside, popping off the caps against the picnic bench as Mr. Parker had taught him.

"Don't go causing any trouble, Maxi."

"It's Max," Uncle Dean said. "Don't call him that."

Over the summer, Mr. Parker had moved from calling him Maxi Pad to Maxi, but he never made it to Max.

He plopped down in the green Adirondack under the kitchen window so he could hear the radio and took a gulp of his Coke. The Cubs were playing the Reds, and he thought about the home run he'd seen Johnny Bench hit at the game yesterday, over the stands and onto the street. A kid had tried to throw the ball back, but he couldn't loft it over the stadium wall.

The August sun had already set. He took the glass jar off the picnic table and headed into the yard to collect lightning bugs. Mr. Parker had shown him how to do this as well, and he always washed the dead bugs out of the jar each week. The challenge wasn't in catching the bugs, Max had discovered, but in snatching each new one fast enough to keep the others from escaping. He'd caught eight the previous Friday, a record that was questionable only because of the extra inning the Sox needed to beat the Angels. If he could break that record, he was sure the Cubs would win.

The ball game was tied in the eighth inning, the poker game was winding down, the losers looking more frustrated with each hand. Max chased the record-breaking bug, but his belly was swollen, three Cokes sloshing around as he moved, making it difficult for him to put in much effort. A chair slapped against the linoleum in the kitchen, and he stopped in time to see Mr. Parker step between his uncle and another man, Mr. Ingersoll. The Cubs game was turned up so he could hear it in the yard, and the voices from inside mixed with the crowd noise, producing an unintelligible rumbling. Mr. Ingersoll was pointing at Dean, and Mr. Parker turned his head to push him back. At the same time, Dean swung a fist over the man's shoulder, smashing Ingersoll in the face. He staggered backward a few steps and fell down against the refrigerator, blood running from his nose.

Max stood with the jar at his side, bugs flying out of the open container. He watched Mr. Parker help Ingersoll up while Dean swept his winnings into his pouch and walked onto the porch. Mr. Ingersoll had given him a stack of his son's comic books a few weeks ago. Max didn't like comics, but he liked Mr. Ingersoll and couldn't imagine why his uncle would want to hit him. Dean blocked the glow from the porch light just as Max saw Mr. Parker hand Ingersoll a package of frozen vegetables for his nose.

"You out there, Max?"

"Uh-huh."

"What kind of response is that? Come on, we're going home."

Dean huffed, breath coming out in quick snorts that made his mustache flutter, and Max lagged behind, partly unable to keep up with him and partly afraid to get too close to his uncle's swinging arms. Dean walked through the kitchen and up the stairs, flipping off lights along the way. "You can listen to the end of the game if you want. But after that, lights out. We've got an early day tomorrow."

✳

"You gotta hear this." Billy read a paragraph from the second chapter of *Circumstantial Evidence*. It was drizzling outside, and the wipers skidded across the windshield. Uncle Dean had preached appearances—his cars always gleamed with fresh coats of wax—but otherwise, his favorite words were Deferred Maintenance.

Max hunched over the wheel, peering between the rain-streaked marks on the windshield, and Billy continued reading.

"Hell, why don't I go back to the beginning?"

The story began like most detective novels, introducing the narrator, the crime, and the setting. Dean always wrote about Chicago, but he never used a detective more than once. *I don't know how people use the same character over and over again. Must be like a marriage,*

135

waking up to the same person every day. It was raining at the beginning of the book—it was always raining during the murder scene, it seemed—and as Billy read about the sheet of "sharp, tack-like" drops that bombarded the narrator, the rain increased outside as well.

"Damn. I mean, are you listening to this. *This* is writing. Your uncle couldn't have been sick when he was writing this. No way. What happened to him?"

"Heart attack. He was at his weekly card game, and he leaned back to stretch. He tipped over backward and was dead by the time he hit the floor."

"Run in your family?"

"I'm not sure. I don't talk to my parents much anymore."

Billy was practically shouting now as waves of rain blasted against the car so hard Max was afraid the roof would cave in. The wipers had been slowing for some time, and just as he noticed this, they stopped, two parallel lines pointing accusingly at the heavens.

"We have to pull over."

"In this storm?"

"Unless you want to climb out on the windshield."

Max turned the car off, and they sat parked on the muddy shoulder, the road obscured by rainwater and the glare of the inside light on the fogging windshield.

"What now?"

"Keep reading."

Billy looked over at him. He pushed back the seat to stretch his legs, maneuvering his feet between the pedals.

"I can't believe you didn't read any of this."

Max shrugged, realizing he hadn't even read the title when he found it in his uncle's desk.

He could see Billy staring at him out of the corner of his eye, but he didn't return the look. Instead, he closed his eyes, remembering Uncle Dean at the train station the morning after he broke Mr. Ingersoll's nose. He hugged Max tightly, the smell of aftershave and hair oil enveloping him almost as much as his uncle's body. Dean slipped something in his pocket. "For the road," he said when Max fumbled at the twenty-dollar bill. He crumpled it in his hand, feeling its inky stiffness give way, and tried not to cry.

The loudspeaker announced his train, and Dean leaned over him, taking his shoulders in his two large hands. "Don't worry, kiddo. Everything's going to be okay."

He thought about that the whole way home, worried his uncle assumed he was scared of the train ride. He'd never been away from home before that summer, and he'd worked hard not to act like a baby. When the train arrived in Harrisburg and he stepped down onto the platform, he saw his mom standing by herself in the waiting room above, waving enthusiastically. *Everything's going to be okay*, he reminded himself.

As he sat in the car, Billy's droning receding in the background, he remembered how wobbly he felt as he walked off the train. He wasn't sure what he'd expected to feel when he got home, but he knew this wasn't it. He looked back at the train, at the window he'd sat next to, wishing he could get back on, wishing he could ride to the next stop, the next city, where he wouldn't know anyone, where no one would be expecting him.

The dome light flickered as he turned the key in the ignition. He flipped the wiper lever to no effect, then switched on the headlights.

"You're going to wear down the battery."

"I can't drive if I don't turn on the car."

"You can't drive in this. You said so yourself."

"Back up a couple of pages. I drifted off."

Billy read haltingly, losing his place every time he looked up to make sure they were still on the road, but Max kept the car between the painted lines, both hands squeezing the steering wheel. The rain was letting up, drops dribbling down the windshield instead of splattering against it, and he sped up. The silhouettes of the fields passed in a blur of rain and speed, and Billy's voice evened out again, regaining its rhythm.

Wallace dropped his snub-nosed revolver to the ground and kicked it away from the man holding the gun to his back. The noise echoed down the long hallway. The dead man's .45 was in his front jacket pocket, but he couldn't pull it out and squeeze off a round in time. For now, though, he had the upper hand as long as he didn't turn around. He knew his eyes would give away whatever plan he hit on, and he didn't want this creep to see it coming when he decided to act.

They drove on, through the one-stoplight towns, the rain falling steadily until Merriman, where the sky cleared all at once, as though they had just come out of a tunnel. The stars were bright above them, and the moon crept from behind the last cloud. Billy read faster, pages turning more quickly as the ending approached.

"If you kill me, you're as good as dead yourself. The police will know you did it."

"Nice try, but you can't scare me like you did Fowler."

He remembered the empty look on young Fowler's face when he shot him in the chest, then his faintly wheezing breath. Suddenly, he knew what to do. He took a step back, forcing the nose of the pistol into his back, and wheeled around, clobbering his nemesis on the side of the head.

The road was empty now, and Max recognized the names of the towns they passed. He slowed down, gauging his speed according to the number of pages still in Billy's lap.

"What's wrong?"

"Nothing. I want to hear the end before I get home."

He wasn't sure why that mattered, but it felt good telling Billy what to do.

Billy turned to the last page, and Max forgot about the trip and everything around them, just as he'd done as he walked toward his mother at the station. And when the end finally came, he forgot what had come before just as quickly as he'd forgotten life with his own family intact, as quickly as he'd forgotten what it felt like to have someone sitting next to him as he drove through the night.

The road rushed up in front of him, and he slowed down, afraid they would collide with the pavement. He drove on, past the Welcome to Hopkins sign, Billy silent at his side.

"Your uncle was some writer." Billy looked up from the pages in his hand, brow furrowed. "You weren't kidding about going west. Where are we?"

"This is where I live," Max said.

"No shit? You live in the middle of nowhere."

"So why did you stay with me this long if you didn't want to end up here?"

"Fuck if I know." Billy paused to stare out the window. "Guess I thought you needed the company."

"I stopped to help *you*, remember."

"Sure you did. You got a bus station around here?"

"Not for another forty miles." Roundtrip, he knew it would take him a good ninety minutes to get Billy to the station and back. Still that might be better than what he'd just thought of. He said it anyway: "You could stay with me. For the night."

"I told you you were lonely." Billy smiled. "I ain't into—"

"Neither am I. And I'm not lonely." Billy's eyes sparkled, even in the dark, but Max could still sense the hesitation in his voice when he agreed. And why shouldn't

Billy be puzzled. Max wasn't sure, himself, why he'd invited him in; it just felt right.

Max turned on to his street, the houses on both sides of the road dark, including his own. He always left the porch light on a timer, but even it had gone off by now. He switched off the headlights. The dim parking lights shone against the pavement like a yellow silhouette. As he pulled into the driveway of his tiny rental, he noticed how ordinary it looked, as though anyone might live there, or no one.

*

While he saw his uncle regularly after his parents' divorce, he hadn't been to Chicago in the year preceding the funeral. Dean wasn't much for traveling, so if Max didn't make the trip, he rarely saw the man. Out of superstition or regret, he avoided the house as long as he could, until after the reading of the will, which gave everything to him. Finally, he had to go inside.

It looked just as it had for years—same outdated furniture, sparsely-appointed kitchen, aging fixtures and appliances. He wandered the rooms as if in a daze.

He ended up in the study on the second floor. He collected the baseballs in one of the empty boxes in the closet. Then he sat at the desk, the one place he'd never been, and looked at the bookshelves lining two walls. They were filled with Dean's books, all forty-seven, with editions in Spanish, French, Italian, as well as the ones from Canada, England, and Australia. There must have been three-hundred in total.

One of their last conversations had taken place in that room, a rarity owing to his uncle's desire for privacy. He had shown Max where he kept his contracts, decades of tax returns, correspondence from editors, other writers, and fans from all over the world. "I don't claim to be a big deal," he'd said, "but I've put in my time and done the best I could." It had the sense of a valediction, though how the man could have known what would happen fifteen months later, Max didn't know.

He remained at the desk, unwilling to go through the drawers, fearing it was too invasive, but finally he turned on the computer. Dean had only recently transitioned away from his typewriter, and when the computer awakened, Max wasn't surprised to find only one document on the desktop. Without reading a word after he opened it, he hit print. He didn't know if his uncle's editor would need to see it, but he, for one, wasn't ready to deal with what he assumed was his final manuscript. Instead, he packed it in a separate box and left the room as quickly as he could. He didn't believe in ghosts, but he also didn't believe in testing fate.

*

Billy wandered around the tiny living room, testing the weight of knickknacks, touching everything, like a child would. He'd offered to take off his shoes, but Max had demurred, fearing the condition of the man's socks and feet. He kept the manuscript nearby, looked back at it whenever he turned away, as though he feared it would disappear.

"It's not much," Max said.

"But it's home, right?"

Without waiting for an invitation, Billy wandered the hallway, into the kitchen and onto the sun porch out back. The house was a cookie-cutter in a cookie-cutter sub-development, just outside of the city limits. When Billy returned, he cocked his head toward the stairs.

"You might as well see everything."

"Got a guest room? I'm starting to fade."

Max nodded. "It's just a pull-out couch."

"I've slept on worse."

Upstairs, Max steered him away from the master bedroom, such as it was, and into the second bedroom. It took Billy less than ten seconds to light on the bookshelves on the far side of the room.

"You bullshitter," he said. "You said you never read him."

"That doesn't mean I didn't buy the books."

Billy turned away to smirk at him. "The creased spines say otherwise."

He wasn't sure why he'd lied to Billy. He owned dog-eared copies of all forty-seven, housed in a glass-enclosed bookcase. He'd read the books so many times he expected the print to fade under the strain. Still, it had seemed important at the time to keep it to himself.

Billy moved to the window, where he looked down on the tiny patch of grass. Max hadn't realized he still had it with him, but Billy held *Circumstantial Evidence* in both hands.

"If you're going to turn in, I'll take that," he said.

Billy looked from him to the manuscript and back again. He studied his hands, shifting the bulk of the manuscript from one to the other as though testing its weight. Max would have to find a rubber band to keep it together.

"I was thinking..."

"Sorry, Billy. I need to keep it with me, on account of the executorship."

"You sure that's the only reason?"

You don't know me that well, he wanted to say, but he didn't want to ruin their tenuous connection. "That's the deal. If you stay here, I keep the book."

"And if I leave?" He studied Max for a long moment before breaking into a smile. "Now I'm bullshitting. I'm not going *anywhere.*"

It sounded ominous. He took the manuscript from Billy's reluctant hands and then showed him where the extra sheets and towels were, buried on the top shelf of the closet. He didn't have many guests.

In his room, with the door closed, he searched for a place to put the book. His bedroom was so small that a bed and nightstand covered one wall. A dresser was the only other furniture. He worked his way from the top drawer, finally finding room in the middle one, the third one down. It contained his work-out clothes—shirts and shorts, swim trunks and windbreaker. He slid the manuscript in the middle of a stack of race t-shirts but realized he was as unwilling to have it out of his sight as Billy had been. He removed it from the drawer.

Then he cleared the alarm clock and biographical tome from the top of the nightstand, leaving them on the floor instead of carrying them across the room, and centered the pages atop the now-empty piece of furniture. He had room on the second shelf for the biography, at least, but President Jackson seemed insignificant compared to his uncle's final work.

He heard Billy in the bathroom next door, the sound of his piss ringing out loudly enough to carry through the wall. The man was humming something slow and mournful, and Max moved closer to the wall to hear it. He couldn't place the tune, imagined it not so much as a love song as a my-love-done-me-wrong blues number. He thought about Billy and his three wives. He thought about his ex-wife. He even thought about his uncle, who had never dated, to his knowledge, never even recycled a protagonist. Forty-seven books with forty-seven different detectives, sometimes cops, sometimes PIs, sometimes innocent people caught in dangerous circumstances.

Billy flushed the toilet, and the humming grew faint as he returned to the guest room, leaving Max alone with his thoughts. He hadn't considered what it would be like to come home knowing that he could no longer pick up the phone and call his uncle, look forward to a trip to Chicago for a ball game and a card night. At least Billy was in the other room. Maybe he could even convince the man to stay awhile.

BORROWED TIME

My wife, Emma, had chosen a dress she'd bought at one of our previous locales—Madison or Denver? —but typically deemed too risqué for our current environs. As a result, she shivered the whole way to my department chair's house. Doug and Barb Culbertson lived two blocks from the visiting writer's bungalow where we were staying. Being warned we were going to *tie one on*, we'd decided to walk even though it was below freezing. I wore a blazer for the first time since my public lecture at the beginning of the school year, on fiction writing as portraiture, and carried two of the better bottles of wine we'd been able to find so far away from civilization. I had an ominous feeling about the night that wasn't allayed by the foggy view of the full moon hanging above the Culbertsons' home or the man's insistence that dinner would be a good time for us to *talk about my future.*

Collier State University was the western-most outpost of the state system. It trained teachers to work in the local, underfunded schools, forestry majors to take on better paying, more dangerous jobs with lumber companies and state parks, and nurses who mainly dealt with the opioid epidemic threatening to overrun much of the region. These students all signed up for fiction writing with the assumption it was an easy A and balked at the workload I'd piled on first semester. I learned from the experience and the blistering student evaluations. In the spring, I cut the page requirements, dropped two novels from the syllabus, and dedicated most of class-time to letting them express their own ill-formed opinions of each other's even more ill-formed stories.

For all of the above reasons, I hadn't been enthusiastic when the chair of the English department and his wife invited us to dinner that February night. I'd been told from the start the visiting gig was for one year only, but the administration was considering granting a tenure-track line that would be ripe for the plucking. Emma was thrilled.

The university had so far accommodated my desire to avoid departmental service, never even sending me the agendas for faculty meetings or bringing up the stipulation I mentor senior theses. Emma approved of setting the bar low, assuming doing so would make the potential tenure-track job less onerous, but I'd always avoided being tied down and wasn't sure I wanted to settle. We'd traveled from one fellowship or visiting professorship to another, sometimes hers, sometimes mine, and made do, in between, on providence—a story placed in a high-paying magazine, a grant from an obscure poetry foundation. But all of a sudden, she talked about putting down roots, mentioned that forty was only two years away, at which point she assured me I'd be remorseful when looking back on all of the wasted opportunities. If Culbertson wanted to offer me a full-time gig, I'd smile and accept.

The Culbertsons lived at the nicer end of our neighborhood, in a two-story colonial that was evidence of Barb's job as CFO of a nearby insurance company. Doug had published three well-regarded books on southern literature, but university presses and a position as department chair wouldn't bankroll a house like theirs.

"Are you sure this is it?" Emma said.

"He said 3248."

"Still... I mean..."

"Slow down on the poetic erudition. I can't keep up."

"Here we go," she said, then squeezed my arm tighter. "Just laugh at all his jokes, flirt with the missus, and we'll leave with that job in our back pocket."

"Your dress is too tight for pockets."

"Come on." She walked up the front steps and rang the bell, which chimed two deep, bass notes.

"Why am I nervous?"

"I told you, time is ticking. You're not getting any younger." She smiled up at me, then added, "No pressure."

Barb opened the door, greeting us with hugs that lingered longer than expected, considering I'd met her only twice before. Not knowing what else to do, I bussed her on the cheek and followed her into the living room, where Doug was bent over their stereo, twirling a knob with each hand.

"There you are," he said once he'd stood up.

I had no idea how to respond. "That's some stereo," I said.

"All the way from Italy!"

"It's his baby," Barb said. "He won't even let Chandra dust it. Does it himself twice a week. Do you think he lifts a finger to clean anything else?"

"You have a lovely home," Emma said, offering the two bottles of wine for inspection.

"Thank you. Doug, have you opened a bottle yet?"

"In the dining room," he murmured. A blues singer's voice emerged from the speakers so clearly, I caught myself looking around for him. "You know Jimmy Higginbottom? Wonderful old guy. I met him one year at the Faulkner conference. His parents were sharecroppers who needed him in the fields, so he stopped school after fifth grade. The legend goes that he can't read, but he told me the truth. The record label likes its musicians *authentic*, so he fakes illiteracy. Clever man."

Barb returned with a decanter of red wine the size of a jug of moonshine, which she handed to her husband. His shoulder strained at the weight. He poured four hefty glasses of the stuff and passed them around. "To a long, profitable relationship," he said.

"I'll drink to that," Emma said.

Barb nodded. "Cheers."

"Don't leave me out," I said, clinking glasses with everyone. "If we're going to do this, let's *do* it." Even I didn't know what I'd meant. The beers I'd had to calm my nerves while Emma was getting ready must have hit me harder than I'd thought.

Doug smiled. "Indeed," he said, steering Emma toward the dining room. His hand was on her back, index finger straying onto the bare skin above her little black dress. "Colin," he said, "why don't you help Barb. In the kitchen?"

I followed her through the dining room and into their kitchen, where an assortment of covered hotel pans sat on an island in the middle of the room.

"Does Emma cook?" she said. "She looks resourceful, is why I ask."

"We both do. A bit. We eat out a lot."

"I ordered all of this from the French place in town. Don't tell her." She placed a hand on my arm. "It'll be our little secret."

The hand stayed on my arm as she guided me around the room, pointed out the hors d'oeuvres we would begin with—foie gras, some kind of marmalade, and bread—and the salad and Provençal rack of lamb to follow. "Dessert is in the fridge. *I* don't even know what it is. I asked them to surprise us!" She released my arm and handed me a glass platter, which I held while she arranged the hors d'oeuvres. "My God," she said, "I didn't even ask if you're vegetarian. You aren't, are you?" She jabbed the tongs in the air between us.

"If you can hunt it," I said, "we'll eat it."

We carried the dishes into the dining room, where Doug loomed above Emma, seated at the foot of the table, showing her something on his phone. "And this is the wall in his study where he outlined the plot. Just fascinating, being able to see the man's mind at work.

Now that so much has been squirreled away, it's one of the few places in the house you can truly feel his presence."

"Let's not talk shop tonight, Douglas. You know how you drone on." Barb widened her eyes at me as she said this.

"Whatever you say, my dear." Once we'd seated ourselves, Doug continued. "Anyway, I'd much rather hear about Colin's work. It's not every day we have a living writer in our midst."

Emma picked up her fork, holding it suspended while she corrected him. "You had Dorothy Paulson here last year, didn't you? She's a marvelous poet."

"*Yes*," he drew out the word. "But not the friendliest woman. Between us, she didn't make the most of her role, did she Barb?"

"A bit chilly, if you ask me." She passed the bread to her husband. "I don't think the students cared for her much, either."

"Dreadful evaluations."

I couldn't help swallowing hard. It would have taken but a few clicks for Doug to come upon *my* dreadful ones from last fall.

"You, on the other hand," he said, stabbing his fork in the air in my direction, "well, I'll admit, I had my doubts at first. That lecture was... peculiar. But you've blossomed since then."

I'd considered the lecture, which I'd previously given at a low-residency program and at a writers' retreat in

Minnesota, the high point of my stay. It had gone over well at both places. An editor had asked me to send it to her, though I hadn't heard back yet about publication.

By the time we'd decimated the hors d'oeuvres, the second bottle of wine had been decanted, and Doug had gone around the table filling glasses. As before, he'd poured to within an inch of the top of the glasses, and this time, partially lubricated, I couldn't help saying, "I like the way you work a bottle, Dr. C."

Emma blushed but Barb didn't bat an eye. "We don't do this often," she said, "but when we drink, we drink!"

My own drinking had escalated since we'd been in Collier, as had my herbaceous habit, once I'd found a local dealer. If we were going to stay, I'd have to slow down, but plenty of time remained before I had to face that possibility.

Barb brought in the rack of lamb, and everyone leaned back from the table in light of its impressive size. We couldn't help giving it pride of place. At first, Barb served us, but we devoured the lamb so quickly she passed the carving knife around the table, along with the dregs of the second bottle of wine. It felt good sharing a meal with these people. While Doug was a bit standoffish at school, referring to everyone by their title, if they had one, or *mister*, as he did with me, he practically rolled up his sleeves and tucked into dinner now that we were away from work.

"You must tell me," he said, "what Hollywood is like."

Several years earlier, a production company had optioned an old story of mine and come up with enough funding to make the movie, which became something of an indie classic. The story wasn't much, just an ill-advised, autobiographical account of a high-school reunion, complete with drunken hijinks and a romp with a classmate, a former track star who'd been out of my league as a teen but had had her head turned by my return as the Published Author. We'd spent most of the official festivities holed up in her hotel room, making use of all of the flat surfaces and a few of the others as well. I dashed off most of the story, hungover, on the plane ride back and put it in a drawer for a year before revising and publishing it. I've always been suspicious of things that arrive too easily.

The money had come in handy. Though I'd published three books, each one had sold worse than the previous one, and I'd made the publishing rounds, going from two New York houses to a Midwestern press. The last book had saddled me with the Writers' Writer label, commercial poison, so when the visiting writer gig arrived unbidden in my in-box, it had felt like a lifeline. Emma and I gave notice, packed our apartment in San Jose a month early, and arrived in Collier before the all-expenses-paid writer's bungalow was ready for us. Like my reunion jaunt, we spent much of the time before the previous visiting writer vacated in the hotel room, making love with a frequency that recalled our early days together. We were that optimistic.

"Doug is working on a book about Modernist writers' interactions with the film world," Barb said, "so this isn't just idle questioning."

I smiled at Barb and looked around the table. We were all such wonderful friends all of a sudden. "Not much to tell. They offered me more to write the screenplay, but what the hell do I know about that?"

"You must have at least *one* story."

I looked at Emma and waited for her approval. We both knew what my *one story* was, but I'd never told it, seeing how it was actually *her* story. She finished her wine and shrugged.

"I sense intrigue," Barb said, looking from one of us to the other.

"No secrets at this table, you two."

"Go ahead," Emma said.

"They had enough money to fly us out for pre-production, so one night, while I was up in the director's hotel suite sharing notes about a draft of the script, Emma waited downstairs, in the lobby. It was supposed to be a quick meeting. A tweak here, a tweak there. But that man can *talk*, and once he started, I thought we were going to miss our dinner reservation. Emma finally got bored and went to the bar for a drink." I looked at her again. If we'd had time, I would have taken her out of the room and gotten written consent, but under the circumstances, I settled for a nod.

"Go on," Doug said. He'd pushed his plate toward the middle of the table, next to the detritus of the lamb.

He was looking not at me but at Emma. He had the same look on his face he'd had when his wife had brought out the main course.

"While Emma's sitting at the bar, one man after another comes up to her, a few minutes apart, and asks to buy her a drink, if she knows a good restaurant, that sort of stuff. She blows them all off, even waggles her wedding ring at a few of them. One guy won't take no for an answer, peppers her with questions, and she keeps shaking her head. She even looks for the bartender, but she's at the other end of the bar, ignoring what's happening. Finally, the guy blurts out, 'I just want to know your rates.'"

I paused then and waited for the story to sink in. Collier was a long way from civilization, based on how long it took for them to put two and two together.

Doug laughed, covering his mouth with his napkin, and his wife said, "How embarrassing. What did you do?"

"I told him he couldn't afford me," Emma said. "Thankfully, Colin showed up right as the creep was leaving." She brushed hair out of her face and then added, "I haven't worn those boots since."

"My dear," Doug said, "you are a delight."

Later, once we'd finished the poached pears, petit fours, and a third bottle of wine, we retired to the living room, where Doug cued up another album. This one I recognized from an English Department mixer. It was a live album, blistering cuts interspersed with the old blues man's ribald stories and jokes.

156

"What are you writing now?" Barb said.

"I'm tinkering with a novel," I admitted. "It's coming slowly, but I go to the desk every day and put in my time." I knew this made me sound too noble. In reality, I spent more time staring out the window at the winter birds in the backyard, puffing on a joint, or answering email. I didn't make a habit of smoking-up while I wrote, but these were difficult times.

"You make it sound like prison," Doug said, waving his wineglass in my direction. It was already half-empty.

"He's dramatic," Emma said, taking my hand. "If he drinks much more, he'll be talking about opening a vein."

I accepted the top-up Barb offered. "I don't know why, but I'm having trouble adjusting here. I've never had this problem before." I felt guilty admitting this to these people, felt the pressure Emma applied to my hand after I'd said it as an indication I should feel even worse. "I'm grateful, don't get me wrong. But we've moved around a lot, and some settings are more conducive than others. Not like Emma. She churns out poems like a machine."

"A poetry machine? How wonderful." Doug took a large gulp of wine. "I appreciate your honesty. I know we're a little more... out-of-the-way than you're used to, but it has its rewards. Now, how about we open one of the bottles you brought?"

I hadn't realized I'd drained my glass, as had everyone else. I looked at Emma. She had the same glassy-eyed stare I assumed I had as well, based on the way the room had begun to sway before me. Doug and Barb looked none the worse for wear, Doug striding across the room in search of another bottle, Barb humming to the music in the background.

When he returned, Doug said, "We should do a little business, I'm afraid." He looked to his wife, who feigned a pout even better than my niece could when she didn't get her way. "The department has been trying for ages to convince the powers that be to open another tenure-track line. The visiting writer position is endowed, so we can't offer it as leverage. But seeing how all of your courses are at capacity, with longer waitlists than almost any in the entire school, I was able to make the case for expanding the writing program. If you're interested in helping me do this, in taking on more of a leadership role, we could certainly use you."

I looked to Emma, who had a bigger smile on her face than she had during the story I'd told about her at dinner. She squeezed my hand once again, a far friendlier action this time, and nodded more vigorously than the basketball players who tried to stay awake through my 9-AM section.

"I'm flattered," I said. "But I'll need to think about it. I'm not sure I'm the administrative type."

"It wouldn't be a full-blown admin position. You'd develop a few new courses and help me select the visiting writer each year. Maybe judge a few awards. Nothing too onerous, I imagine."

"What Colin should have said was, 'thank you,'" Emma said. "Neither of us has ever had an offer like this, so we'll need to discuss it before he responds."

"Time is ticking, as they say."

No kidding. I'd already applied for half-a-dozen VAPs for the next year. None had panned out. I figured something would come up, but I couldn't help feeling a little panicked.

Barb interrupted my thought process. "We'd love to have you around—you too, Emma. It's not often, in a small town, that you feel a connection to another couple. And Doug being the chair of the department only makes it more difficult for us."

Emma nodded again, but I felt frozen in place. The wine had hit me full force, and I wasn't sure if I could have made my way out of the house if it had caught fire just then. I could feel my ears burning, as they did when I had too much to drink, and my tongue had turned to sandpaper. Emma seemed fine, though her tolerance wasn't any better than mine, so I knew she was trying harder than I was to seem in control.

"It's been a lovely evening," Barb continued. "We're rarely able to relax and unwind like this."

"We should probably be going," Emma said.

"On the contrary!" Doug said, hopping to his feet. "Have another glass. I have port in the basement, if you're interested."

"I don't have room for another drop," Emma said.

"We've sated them, Douglas." Then, Barb added, "We do have one more thing we'd like to show you."

I anticipated a trip to Doug Culbertson's renowned library of signed first-editions, or a dull recounting of a couples' vacation, complete with mementoes and a scrapbook. Instead, Doug walked over to the armoire in the corner, which housed a modest flat-screen television.

"I think you'll like this," he said. "At least, we hope you will."

Barb turned out the lights, which made me feel even more disoriented. My head seemed to detach from my body, rising to the ceiling like a helium balloon, from which vantage point it swayed in the breeze and looked down on the scene below. I could barely make out Emma's features though she was still right next to me.

"This isn't the point where you recruit us into your cult, is it?" she said. She let out an uneasy laugh.

"Not at all, my dear. We just want to share something with you."

The screen lit up, illuminating the top half of the room. On it, I watched as someone trained a camera on a bedroom, two people standing in the foreground, naked except for black, Mardi Gras-style eye masks. The woman was hard to look away from. She was full-chested, slight of waist, and long of leg. She was beautiful. She was Barb Culbertson.

The man stood with his hands on his hips, in his best Superman pose, obviously proud of the enormous erection, emphasized by his shaved pubic area, aimed just above the camera. His balls had already contracted. He was locked and loaded, as my old college roommate would have said. And, in keeping with the woman's identity, he was clearly Doug Culbertson, chair of the department and my boss.

"Umm..." I said, but nothing else would come out.

"Just watch." The voice was so breathy I wasn't sure who'd spoken.

The couple cavorted, standing and prone, for what felt like thirty minutes, touching, licking, sucking, and fucking. At a certain point, Doug had removed the camera from the tripod and carried it with him, shooting from his own point of view, capturing every inch and orifice of his wife's body for digital posterity.

"What is this?" Emma said. "I mean... I don't know *what* I mean!"

"Do you like it?" This time I could tell Barb was speaking. She'd phrased it as a question but clearly expected only one answer.

"Umm..." I said, again. I tried to find Emma's eyes in the dark but only saw two shining pinpoints, focused on the screen. "We should go."

Though the events depicted in my Hollywood short story had happened before Emma and I had met, she was still touchy about it. Whenever the movie appeared on the menu for our streaming service, she'd leave the room, as though I was enough of an idiot to ogle a twenty-something ingénue's full-frontal scenes in front of my wife. I feared the kind of blow-up we'd gone through the first time someone made a joke about the movie in her presence.

Doug paused the video. His wife's ass, filmed from behind, filled the screen.

"Could you maybe turn that off?" I said.

"It's in good fun," he said. "Isn't she beautiful?"

Barb stood and joined him in front of the TV, blocking most of the digital version of her body. I couldn't help assessing her in a way I hadn't previously. Yes, she looked as good, in a different way, as she did in the video. Her skirt covered the legs that had spread wide for her husband, and her breasts, which he'd slapped with abandon, were corralled beneath a thick sweater, but the video had left nothing to the imagination. I had to strain not to superimpose that image onto the real thing.

"We really need to go," I said. Then I added, "Don't we?"

"Mm hmm," Emma said, but her eyes stayed transfixed on the tableau before us. "We could stay a bit longer."

"I think we should leave."

"Listen to your wife," Doug said. "We could have some fun together."

"You're swingers?"

"It's the twenty-first century," Barb said. "Nobody uses that term anymore."

"Whatever the term is, count us out."

Doug shook his head. "I'm not sure Emma agrees with you."

She finally turned toward me, half of her face illuminated by the screen, the other half, the one closest to me, and the door, in shadow. "It could be interesting."

"I saw the way you looked at me when you first came in," Barb said.

"There was no look. I was being polite!"

"I meant your wife."

Emma bored a hole through me with her drunken, pinpoint eyes. I didn't know what to do, how to reach her in this state. True, I'd looked forward to some drunken cavorting after the party, but I didn't want to sleep with my boss's wife, or my boss, for that matter.

"I'm leaving," I said, then struggled to my feet. My legs almost gave out as I rose, and they weren't much steadier once I put my full weight on them. "Did you drug the wine?" I said.

Barb laughed.

Doug shook his head and said, "That would be a violation of trust. And, may I say we *trust* you won't share this with anyone, regardless of what happens next?"

"What happens next is that I walk out of here and scrub this whole night from my mind." I couldn't imagine who I would tell. I barely knew the other faculty, only saw them in the copy room when I dashed off a hand-out before workshop. Just in time printing, I called it. Now, my one connection in Collier had made it impossible for me to ever look him in the eye.

"You know," he said, seeming to read my mind. "Life can go on as before. You can teach your classes, we can speak in the hallway, and you might still get that tenure-track position."

"Might?"

"Collegiality is a big part of the decision."

"Meaning?"

Emma stood next to me. But she didn't take the arm I offered. "Colin can leave if he wants to," she said, "but I'm staying."

"Good girl."

With that, I turned on my heel as confidently as I could and negotiated my way around the furniture and to the front door. I paused for a moment, but once I knew Emma wasn't following, I opened it and walked into the cold February night.

The university was in the mountains, which meant twice the snowfall and temperatures that hovered in the twenties until spring break. I turned up the collar on my blazer and fought my way through the wind that rattled the skeletal tree branches.

I couldn't believe Emma had stayed behind. Actually, I could. She'd been proudly bi- when we'd met, though she'd never acted on impulses for anyone other than me, regardless of their sex, in the eight years we'd been together. She'd always been better than me at keeping secrets: she never revealed her work-in-progress until it was publication-ready, never told me what she did all day, beyond writing, while I was at the university. Most of all, never talked about her past—what she'd done before we'd met, where she'd lived, whom she'd dated. It had taken two years for her to introduce me to her parents. And almost as long before I learned where she'd gone to college. This night might become another thing I never knew anything about. By the time I'd made it up our front walk, I knew I couldn't let that be true.

＊

I don't know what time Emma returned. I tried to wait for her but passed out close to one a.m. Looking back on it from my hungover state in the morning, I realized Doug and Barb had filled our glasses disproportionately. While it had seemed like we were all drinking at the same rate, Barb was quick to top-off my glass—Emma's too—and much more reserved in serving herself and her husband.

I awoke with the kind of headache that left me weak-kneed and parched, head jackhammering and stomach in danger of heaving at any moment. I wished I *would* throw up. But nothing came out when I tried. Emma snored in bed, on her back, while I banged around in the bathroom, changed out of the shirt and tie I'd passed out in, and headed for the kitchen. Light poured in through the French doors taking up much of the back wall, and I fumbled for the sunglasses I kept in my fashionably-distressed leather satchel. Once I'd found them, I poured a glass of orange juice and made coffee, grinding the beans long enough I knew I must have awoken Emma. By the time the coffee finished brewing, I heard her having more success in the bathroom than I'd had.

She emerged twenty minutes later, bobbed hair standing up on one side of her head, robe cinched over bare skin. She was even more woozy than I was. In fact, I'd never seen her look so bad, not even the morning after her bachelorette party—another event of which she never spoke.

"Have fun?"

"I'm so hungover it hurts when the *air* touches me."

"Poetic justice?"

"Tell me another one, since I'm so clearly in the mood."

"You're awfully testy considering..."

She tried out a deep, serious voice, filled with mock-gravitas. *"Considering I stepped outside of the bonds of marriage."*

"Well, yes."

"At least I didn't let Doug and Barb film me." She poured coffee into a white mug—everything in the kitchen was equally white, almost blindingly so under current conditions.

She smiled over the rim of her mug. "It was rather tame, in comparison to your story." She looked at me. "I let them watch me rub one out. With a blanket over my lap. No juicy bits, no penetration. That's all." She took my orange juice and drank half in one greedy gulp. "I might have saved your job."

"That's why you did it?" In my hungover state, I almost believed her. I *wanted* to believe her. But she smiled too broadly for it to be true.

"I shouldn't drink red wine. It makes me... You know."

"Clearly," I said.

"What do you say we never speak of this again? Like Doug said, go on as before, like nothing happened."

"That's what you want?"

"It's not like I'm going to do it again."

"You're sure?"

"Right now, I don't ever want to see a wine bottle, let alone drink from one. Not to mention what Doug did to Barb after you left..."

"Enough," I said. I turned my mug's handle away from me. Without food soon, the coffee would upset my stomach even more. "I know this job is important to you..."

"I wish you took it as seriously."

"I don't want to create an expectation that—never mind." I didn't want to think about the possibility of a repeat performance, or of ever seeing the Culbertsons again under any circumstances.

"But it's okay for you to relive your dirty weekend any time you want. That movie isn't even any good!" She winced as she raised her voice.

"I didn't even know you back then."

"I don't need the world throwing that—"

"Not like masturbating in front of my boss. Nothing wrong with that."

"You're a prude," she said. "You got drunk, freaked out, and ran away from our last chance. *I* picked up the pieces."

I hate arguing. Out of boredom, we'd done more of it than usual since we'd arrived in Collier. But this was one I truly did not have the stomach for. It seized up just then. By the time I returned from the bathroom, Emma had left for her writing studio in the attic. I didn't have the energy to follow her.

The strange thing was that once we cooled down and recovered from our epic hangovers, we actually did what Emma recommended. I never mentioned that Friday night, and Emma, sensing a truce, no longer glared at me every time *The Class of '94* played. I got my job, finished my book, and earned some decent reviews. Emma became the next visiting writer at Collier State, during which time she published yet another collection, which won enough prize money to keep her going for several more years. Three years later, Doug was let go for sending students what he thought were anonymous dick pics. Based on what I'd seen, they must have been some pics.

I've put the incident behind me. I only think of it on those nights when I'm sitting up alone in our kitchen, drinking too much whiskey, and reading Emma's email. It took me weeks of trying out incorrect passwords, but now that I'm in, I don't plan on getting caught.

THE SOPRANO AT MIDLIFE

"We can still turn back," Everett said.

"It's been three years." Rosalind reached past her husband and rang the doorbell. "Have we ever gone three months without visiting *your* family?"

"That's not the point. It's just—my book."

His book. That's all she heard anymore. She tuned him out and squinted at the door, the sun reflecting off the glass panels. She listened for footsteps, but the sound of the Pacific was too loud, so she rang the doorbell again.

"...stressful time. And Geoff needs that article for *Quarterly Renaissance Studies.*"

"I thought that's why we paid to bring an extra suitcase, for your research."

He sighed.

"What?"

The door opened before he could answer, Celia, her sister, standing in front of them, the sun illuminating her tanned skin and blond highlights.

"We were starting to worry." She beamed at each of them, said, "What's up, Doc?" to Everett, a running joke between them, and reached forward to hug her older sister. She was taller than Rosalind remembered, and they stood shoulder-to-shoulder as they embraced. She'd been a chubby kid, but as Rosalind hugged her, all she felt was muscle and bone.

"The rental counter lost our reservation."

"It's not a reservation," Everett said. "It's a *preference*. Our preference was for a compact, but they *preferred* to make us wait in line for fifty minutes and give us that." He pointed toward the sedan with the heated seats and the light-sensitive tinted windows as though it were a chariot whose horses they'd have to feed and stable.

Rosalind felt like a beggar, standing on the front stoop, bags in hand, waiting to be invited in, while her husband rehashed his complaints about the rental car company, once again threatening to write a letter. He shared her mother's unquestioned faith in the power of the written word.

Celia nodded and wrinkled her brow in all the right places, then interrupted the first time he paused. "Come in," she said, without offering to help with the luggage. She turned toward the back of the house and called, "They're here, Park. Come take their bags."

The entryway was bare, containing only a small table on three spindly legs. A green ceramic bowl with a jumble of keys and coins sat atop it. Glossy hardwood floors stretched from the door to the back of the house, where an unbroken expanse of glass overlooked a private beach. The ocean was choppy, the water gray in the early-evening light. The open plan allowed her to see the living and dining rooms and the kitchen from the foyer. Everything looked perfectly arranged, albeit sparsely furnished—two semi-circular sectional couches in the living room, a black metal table and chairs, gleaming stainless-steel appliances in the kitchen. The kind of place a director would use to imply a character's antiseptic, deadened life, nothing like what she expected from her sister.

The sliding glass door in the kitchen opened and a man in khaki shorts and a black tank top came toward them, putting on a white linen shirt. "Sorry, love, I didn't hear them pull up," he said. His words ran together, and Rosalind had to concentrate to understand him. He headed straight for her. "Let me take those." He reminded her of a statue she'd seen at the national museum in Rome in high school, when she'd accompanied her mother to a conference. *Hermes Loghion.* She'd drawn a rough sketch of it in the journal she'd taken for all the wonderful insights she'd expected to have but hadn't. Park had the same tight, blond curls and soft jaw line, same broad, muscular shoulders and pectorals, but with a slight potbelly pushing at his tank top.

"Welcome," he said, enfolding her in a tighter embrace than her sister had. "I've heard all about you," he murmured.

"You, too, Everett." He turned to her husband. "Fuck that. Give me a hug, mate." He slipped past her husband's outstretched hand and wrapped both arms around him, more intimate than the one-armed hugs Everett and his brothers exchanged at holidays. "That's more like it."

"Where are the sprogs?" he said when no one else spoke.

"I told you they weren't bringing them," Celia said.

"They're with Everett's parents."

Park frowned. "Too bad. I love kids." He gathered most of the bags in his arms and said, "Go out on the patio. I've got these."

Outside, a breeze blew off the Pacific, buffeting the umbrella above the glass-topped table. A stone bar and grill sat to the left of the table, while straight ahead, a private boardwalk led to the beach a few yards away. Sand dusted the tile floor, and a solo guitar played a jazz riff over the speakers hidden beneath the roofline.

"This place is amazing," Everett said, dropping into a lounge chair near the bar.

"Not bad for a bach, but I wish you'd visit us in New Zealand."

"A what?" Rosalind said.

"Bach? You know, a vacation place."

Everett laughed. "Pretty soon you'll be offering us a cuppa and some biscuits."

"She's not in England."

"He's right, sis. We use a lot of English expressions."

We, as though she'd lived there all her life, not grown up in Baltimore and lived with them in Indiana until three years earlier. She'd been their part-time nanny

172

and a part-time yoga instructor until she'd gone to Christchurch to study with a famous yoga teacher.

"You look good," Celia said to her.

"I've put on weight."

"You've always had a great figure, like Jane Russell."

"She was something," Everett said. "Have you seen *Macao*, with Robert Mitchum?"

Before either of them could answer, Park returned with a platter piled with food for the grill, and Rosalind realized that, without meaning to, she'd been waiting for him to return before getting comfortable. "You haven't gotten them drinks," he said. "What kind of hostess are you?"

"I'll take a beer," Everett said, "if you've got anything good."

"Beer!" Park pointed a wooden skewer at him.

"Now you've done it." Celia smiled and shook her head.

"Beer's for students and laborers. We only drink wine here."

Rosalind leaned toward her husband. "His family owns a winery."

"I forgot."

"We had to go to four stores to find it," Celia said.

"We make the best fucking Sauvignon Blanc you've ever tasted, but if it isn't from California, people here act like it's toxic. Grab us a bottle, Marie. I want to put the food on."

"Marie?"

"Celia's his grandmother's name. He calls me by my middle name."

Park waited until she'd gone in the house to elaborate. "The first time we were in bed, I'm lying on top of her with her ankles by my ears, and I'm about to bust. But then I say, 'Oh, Celia,' and it makes me think of Nana." He turned to Everett. "That was the end of that."

Celia returned, a chilled bottle in one hand and a stack of plastic cups in the other. "So help me, you weren't telling that story."

"Nana's ninety, with varicose veins *everywhere* and these whiskers sprouting from her chin long enough you can *braid* them. As soon as I recovered, I told her I'd call her anything she wanted so long as it wasn't Celia."

"Do you expect us to call you that, too?" Rosalind said.

Park responded before her sister could. "Only if you interrupt us in the bedroom."

Everett sipped the wine and said, "Not bad. Kind of fruity."

"Gooseberries," Park said without turning from the grill. Thick slabs of fish sizzled when he put them over the heat. "The Aussies go crazy for that fruity shit, but we know how to temper it. You notice that other flavor, the one that hits in the back of your throat? Asparagus. Balances out the berries and keeps it from being too pussy." He looked at Rosalind. "No offense."

"That smells good," Rosalind said. She'd spent the last week thinking of what to say to her sister, but now that she was there, her mind had gone blank. Everything was moving too quickly.

"Most people get too fancy with fish. If you buy the best, all you need is pepper and the tiniest bit of salt. Let the natural flavor do the rest."

"I hope you aren't burning the veggies." Celia said. "He likes them black."

"A nice char never hurt anyone." He removed everything from the grill, squirted lemon juice over it, and arranged it on platters, then brought over skewers of multi-colored bell peppers, squash, pearl onions, and mushrooms, the tuna fillets, and a bowl of steaming couscous with pine nuts and currants mixed in.

"This looks amazing," Everett said. "You didn't have to go to all this trouble."

"I want you to feel welcome. Even in California it's difficult to find places that satisfy the princess over there."

"You're still vegan?" Rosalind said.

"You say that like it's a disease."

"Only asking."

"I wish you'd at least try the tuna. The fatty acids are great for you." He turned to their guests. "You know about omega-3s? You Americans don't get enough of them. Too much omega-6, from poultry and grains, not enough of this stuff." He waved a forkful of tuna around like a conductor with a baton.

175

"Excuse Park. He's obsessive."

"This from the vegan who got up at four AM the day we left to fit in her yoga." He ate a bite of couscous, tongue smacking against the roof of his mouth, then chased it with a swallow of wine.

"She went through a phase," Rosalind said, "where she wouldn't eat anything green, and now she's a vegan?"

"We all change," Celia said.

"Remember when you freaked out because Mom served green chutney for that visiting scholar from India? She was so embarrassed I thought she was going to put you up for adoption."

Celia pursed her lips into a tight smile. "I was six."

"'It looks like slime,'" Rosalind said in a whiny, little-girl's voice. "Dr. Rajnipal almost choked on a piece of cauliflower, he was laughing so hard."

Park looked at Celia before changing the subject. "Do you detox?"

"Not while we're eating."

"Like rehab?" Rosalind said.

"Purging toxins. I eat nothing but fruits and veg for a week every other month. I've got some great supplements—totally natural—I'll show you."

"I tell him if he ate better all the time, he wouldn't have to do that."

"It's no fun always being good. What about you, Everett? Up for a colonic tomorrow?"

"I'll just work on my book."

"Fair play. I read your first one—*Shakespeare in the Cold War*? Brilliant, mate."

"I gave him mine," Celia said. "It took me *months* to get through it. He read it in a weekend."

"You liked it?" Everett put down his fork so he could concentrate on Park's admiration.

"The chapter on *Richard III* in Moscow was choice. I never thought of the political uses of four-hundred-year-old plays."

"That means a lot coming from a fellow writer."

"I'm nothing like you. What're you working on now?"

"Don't get him started," Rosalind said. She turned to her sister and said, "You think Park goes on about fatty acids? Wait until you hear Everett about his book."

"Mom never talks about hers, at least not with me."

"She and Everett disappear for hours, debating the ending of *Measure for Measure*."

"It was *Troilus and Cressida*. And it happened once."

"On Christmas morning. The kids had to wait until lunch to open presents."

"Ignore them, Park," Everett said. "When Celia was living with us, all they did was gang up on me." He tapped a finger against the tabletop, emphasizing the keywords the way he did when reciting a poem. "I'm looking at how film adaptations influence our interpretations of the plays."

"You ought to come with me tomorrow. Get the behind-the-scenes tour."

"I've never been on a movie set."

"How's the film going?" Rosalind said.

"The director's a bit dodgy, thinks he's too good for a kid's movie—"

"The studio thinks it could be the next *Harry Potter*," Celia said.

"That's why they put us up here and are generally kissing my ass. They want a deal on the rights to the other books." Park had written a series about a Scottish boy in the eighteenth century who runs away from home and stows aboard a pirate ship.

"I wish they had shot it on location. Even with the sets, Santa Monica hardly looks like the Barbary Coast." He paused to finish his wine. "The kid who plays Rory's good."

"A year from now, Park will be more famous than that vampire chick," Celia said. "Did you read his latest? I can already see the lines outside the theaters."

"They're for kids, right?"

"Don't mind my husband, the snob," she said. She hadn't read the books either, for the same reason. She'd tried reading the first one to their oldest, Viola, but it had given her nightmares.

"Fair enough. I've toyed with writing one for adults. I have to leave out so much to make them kid-friendly. Like the butt-fucking. When they were at sea, those ships were like bath houses. Can you imagine?"

Celia brought out another bottle of wine. "You're obsessed with that," she said. "He wrote a sex scene for the last one, as a joke on his agent. It was filthy. Literally."

"They didn't have access to high colonics. If you come tomorrow, Everett, you've got to go all the way."

"That's enough about that," Rosalind said. "I'm still eating."

*

After college, Rosalind had moved to New York, where she sang with a fledgling opera company in Fort Greene, equating its geographical proximity to the Metropolitan Opera with her professional goals. Two years later, at twenty-four, fresh from being a finalist in the National Council Auditions, she'd sung the female lead in *Faust*, to moderate acclaim, and with this triumph behind her, she'd gone home for a visit.

Celia had moved back in, having recently withdrawn from one of the state universities owing to a bout of pneumonia. She would drop out of two more schools later, but the novelty of this being the first one coupled with the illness made everyone solicitous. She'd lost twenty pounds while sick, and Rosalind had found it difficult to adjust to this new, slimmer Celia, one who had an interest in macrobiotics and meditation.

Sitting on Celia's bed one afternoon, she flipped through the *Bhagavad-Gita*, pausing only to look at the notations her sister had made in the margins, half-listening to Celia's chatter about traveling through Asia,

179

something that had occurred to her after attending one of the Tibetan Freedom Concerts in D.C.

"Mm," she said after Celia's story about a lightning strike at the concert. She reread a highlighted line: *let not the fruits of action be thy motive; neither let there be in thee any attachment to inaction.* Could dropping out of college and sleeping until ten every day be considered an *attachment to inaction?*

"Are you listening?" Celia said.

"Not entirely," she admitted.

"How many of your recitals have I sat through?"

She put down the book and looked at her sister, on the window seat, her old clothes hanging off her new body. Celia smiled the way she had as a kid after she'd snuck into Rosalind's room and hidden her older sister's algebra book or rearranged her cassette tapes. "Mom has someone she wants you to meet. A PhD student from Toronto. She says he's *brilliant.*"

"Just what I need. An academic who can't find his car in the grocery store parking lot or pay bills on time because he's too busy explicating some sonnet that holds the key to the universe."

Their mother held her graduate seminar at the house, in the two-story library off the dining room, and when the class ended that night, she invited everyone to stay for drinks. She and Celia mingled with the students, five men and three women, and listened to debates about Falstaff and Henry the Fourth, Shakespeare's sonnets versus Donne's. The brilliant Canadian scholar, Geoffrey Watkins, was the center of these discussions, quoting from memory, gesturing wildly with both hands to explain why "Batter my heart" was better than any of Shakespeare's poetry.

"'and bend/ Your force to break, blow, burn and make me new.'" He repeated the verses, more slowly. "Listen to the power in those lines. The combination of religious imagery..."

She caught her mother looking at her, her eyes positively gleaming. She shrugged in response and went to refill her glass. Celia had already disappeared, as usual, leaving her to fend for herself, to be on display, the jewel in their mother's familial crown.

Struggling with the corkscrew, she felt someone come up next to her.

"Can I help?" The man took the bottle from her, twisted the cork back and forth, squeaking as it turned, and gave up. "I think this one's a lost cause."

"Follow me," she said. "We'll get something stronger."

In the kitchen, she got down a bottle of whiskey, poured two glasses, and added ice.

The man sipped carefully, grimaced, then added water. "I'm not much of a drinker," he said.

"What a blowhard." She looked toward the door and the library beyond.

"Guess I'm used to him."

"Does he always go on like that?"

"You've never been in grad school."

He had long, straight hair, pulled back in a loose ponytail, the sides falling out and mingling with neatly trimmed sideburns. She felt the urge to reach out, tuck the errant strands behind his ears, but didn't want to do anything so clichéd. Instead, she stopped his hand from bringing his glass to his lips, leaned forward, and kissed him. He tried to pull back, but she wouldn't let him.

"I have a girlfriend," he said when she finally released him. "She's in the other room."

"She's probably picturing herself screwing the Donne expert right now." Where had this confidence come from? She decided she liked it. "Who needs her."

She stared at him, watching the dilemma play out in his eyes, before he yielded. He was still hesitant, polite, until she forced her tongue between his half-parted lips. A moan escaped from deep in his chest, and he gave in completely.

"I'm Everett," he said as she led him up to her room.

*

"What do you think of Park?"

They were walking through an outdoor arcade north of LA while the men monitored filming on *Rory and the Barbarous Sea Robbers*. She followed her sister from stall to stall, where Celia fingered jewelry and cooed over handmade bags and driftwood art that she found hideous and kitschy.

"He talks a lot."

182

Celia held an organic-cotton blouse in her hand. "When did you become such a bitch?"

"So much for 'absence makes the heart grow fonder.'"

"I could say the same thing." She dropped the blouse on the table and pulled her sister out of the line of traffic. Up close, Rosalind could see the sunspots dotting her sister's forehead. "Last night you looked like Mom, sitting there judging everyone while we tried to have a good time. Lighten up, for fuck's sake."

"I see Park's rubbed off on you."

Celia held her hands out like she wanted to choke her, then walked away. It reminded her of the fights they'd had as kids. They were five years apart, spaced deliberately so that their mother could fit a book in between them—*Deconstructing Ophelia: Shakespearean Heroines After Derrida.*

She caught up to Celia, grasped her arm, surprised by the rigidity of her muscles, the feel of tendons and bone. She was all joints and angles, especially in the slip of a sun dress she wore in defiance of the cool, breezy weather.

"*I sorry,*" she said, mimicking their childhood apology.

Celia ignored her, paid for a silver necklace with a large quartz embedded in it like a talisman.

"Lighten up, Marie," she said, affecting Park's accent. "Quit your wonky whinging."

Her sister snorted. "That was terrible. I thought you were an actress."

"Opera's different. We don't sing in accents."

"Come on. I'll buy you a *sarnie*." She emphasized the last word with Rosalind's fake accent, then directed them to a café across the street from the market.

They looked over the menu, ordered lunch and half a bottle of wine, and watched the shoppers at the market, the seagulls on the pier across the street fighting over scraps. Neither of them said a word until their sandwiches arrived, when Rosalind gave in.

"How's the studio?" Park's family had given her the money to open a yoga studio in Wellington after she'd finished studying in Christchurch.

"I hired two more teachers before we left. I hate to have new people starting when I'm not there, but I couldn't cover all the classes otherwise."

"Are you worried, being gone so long?"

"Worried, no. Neurotic, yes." She wiped hummus from the corner of her mouth. "I call every day, which is a real pain with the time difference. Why are you smiling?"

"When you lived with us, you couldn't balance a checkbook, now you're an entrepreneur. Remember the time—"

"People change."

Rosalind didn't know what else to say. After three years, her store of sisterly reference points had evaporated, so she picked at the potato salad on her plate, separating out the roasted red pepper and eating it one piece at a time.

"Are you singing?"

"I did *Onegin* in Chicago as a replacement, but nothing regular. The kids take up a lot of time."

"They're both in school now."

"They still have to eat and have clean clothes, not to mention that Chicago's seventy-five minutes away and I'm teaching a full slate of lessons."

"Don't get defensive." When she didn't respond, Celia added, "You're so talented."

She'd heard the same thing since she was a teen. She'd given her first recital at fifteen, with a glowing review in the *Baltimore Sun*, then gone on to Eastman, where she'd sung the major mezzo-soprano parts—Carmen and Rosina, in *The Barber of Seville*—and several dramatic soprano roles as well. But sometime after that—when the company in Fort Greene went bankrupt, when she got tired of taking the train twice a month to visit Everett and moved back to Baltimore, when he got the job at Northern Indiana and she got pregnant the first time—her life had gone off course. Now, her sister and Everett were the only ones who used present tense when discussing her talent.

*

Early the next morning, while Celia did yoga on the patio and Everett slept, she sat in the living room, browsing the playlist on the mp3 player she'd found on the kitchen counter. Only a few of the names seemed familiar—Coltrane, Monk, Django Reinhardt—but towards the end of the long list she found highlights from *Rigoletto*. She was about to push play when the front door opened and Park entered, a bicycle hoisted on his shoulder.

"I thought you were sleeping."

He flinched. "Fuck. I didn't see you." He set the bike against the wall, walked past her and into the kitchen. He moved like a movie cowboy, legs apart, on account of the cushioning in his spandex shorts. He had thin, muscular legs, and she watched the contours of his calves bulge and relax with each step. His shoes clacked against the tile like they had taps on the bottom. He took a bottled water from the fridge and joined her in the living room.

"Do you shave your legs?"

"Cuts down on wind resistance. And I like the way it feels."

She couldn't decide if he was kidding or not.

He sighed as he dropped onto the couch opposite her. "One of the great things about this place is that I can get my sweaty body all over the furniture without Marie packing a wobbly. 'I don't want your funk infecting everything,'" he said in a whining American accent. "That looks like mine."

"It was in the kitchen." He waved her away when she held it out. "You like jazz," she said.

He nodded. "You sing opera."

186

"Sometimes."

"I like the tragic stuff—*La Boheme*, *Tosca*. I want to leave feeling rung out. I'm a sadist."

"Great choices. What about *Rigoletto*?"

"You saw that, eh. I found a guitar transcription, thought we might do a duet."

"Celia didn't tell me you play."

"I dabble."

"I haven't sung *Rigoletto* since college."

"I've got the libretto if you need it."

"How about sets and costumes?"

"Rack off. I thought it might be fun."

"Sorry." She scrolled through the playlists again. "Tell me about what you like."

"You mind?" he said, moving next to her. "I'm ponging something awful." He put his hand over hers, so they held the iPod between them. "What do you want to know?"

She ran her finger around the wheel a few times, coming to a stop on one that sounded intriguing—*Ascenseur pour l'echafaud*.

"Fucking brilliant. Miles Davis's soundtrack to a Louis Malle flick. Great title: *Elevator to the Gallows*. Malle convinced him to improvise a score while watching clips in the studio. Jeanne Moreau—she was in it—hung out. There's a great photo of them, Miles playing his horn in her ear."

"Is the film good?"

187

He smiled, showing a row of overlapping bottom teeth. "Never seen it. I like to put it on when I'm walking around and imagine my own version. Dark, rainy streets, *femme fatales* in trench coats looking to fuck me and get me killed. Stupid stuff, really."

"I understand." She let go of the iPod, slipping her hand out from under his. "I should wake Everett. You must have worn him out yesterday."

"The first colonic can take it out of you."

"I can't believe you convinced him to do it."

He tugged at the elastic on one leg of his shorts. "I'm pretty persuasive."

*

She walked down the hall but turned into an empty guest room. From the window, she watched Celia, balanced on one foot, the other leg and her torso parallel to the ground with her top arm pointing toward the sky. Every muscle in her back stood out, contoured like the bark of a tree.

Rosalind couldn't help thinking of Park's Miles Davis story. One Tuesday that winter, she'd taken the train into Chicago for rehearsal at the Lyric Opera. A cold day, even for that month, she wore her full-length coat, swaddled herself in scarf and hat, but when she got off at Millennium Station, she walked down Michigan Avenue toward the Art Institute instead of catching her bus to the Opera. She stopped in front of the Crown Fountain, dry for the winter, and watched the faces projected on its screens. In warmer weather, water would shoot from their lips and kids splashed in the long, narrow pool bookended by the two screens. Now, she stood alone, studying the faces, while a busload of teens waited for the Institute to open.

She'd been listening to Bychkov's *Onegin* every day, studying the performances, but suddenly she needed a change. Another chorus member had recommended an album by a Chicago jazz singer, a song-cycle based on Ovid. This singer's voice was far from operatic, and the lyrics, in English, startled her after two hours of Russian. *I can be fire I can be war I am the daughter of Zeus.* She didn't know what to make of these words; at least opera came with a storyline, dialogue, and characters to connect with. But she kept listening, making up her own story to fit the music, based on the fountain's changing faces.

When the museum opened, she paid her admission, climbed the stairs, and wandered through the rooms of Impressionist and Contemporary Art. She spent the morning there, the album playing on a loop in her ears, and studied the paintings from every angle, stepping as close as security would allow, waiting to move to another canvas until she had an unobstructed view.

She didn't know why she skipped rehearsal, what she hoped to gain from her time at the Art Institute, but she remained until lunch, when the spell passed and she rushed to the Opera in a panic, shattering the morning's calm, and told her lie. An ear infection that required an emergency trip to the pediatrician, a dead cell phone battery. She burrowed among the chorus for the afternoon's rehearsal, ignored whatever discontent had led her astray.

But it came back, once a week at first, then more frequently. She walked the streets, music humming in her ears, bought garish hats and unnecessary pairs of shoes, eavesdropped on cell phone conversations, gradually expanded her circuit. Lincoln Park, the Gold Coast, Old Town. She couldn't help herself. She singled out people to follow, created complicated lives of hidden intrigue for them—affairs, insider trading, a second family they'd abandoned on a farm in Iowa—forgetting the stories once the people disappeared into office buildings, up the stairs to El platforms.

After the final performance of *Onegin*, the fourth one Everett had attended, the General Director told her she wouldn't be asked back. "We have a challenging season planned for next year," he said. "We need reliable performers." He cut her off before she could respond. "You don't seem to *want* to be here," he said. "We can't have that."

For the first time, she realized she couldn't argue with that assessment.

✳

The sun dropped below the horizon, and Celia lit candles that flickered in the breeze stirring the sand on the patio. They'd piled their dishes in the center of the table, next to the three bottles of wine they'd finished. She couldn't remember ever eating so well, not just the tuna fillets but a spicy shrimp-and-soba noodle dish the previous night and the empanadas—some chorizo-filled, others with spinach and bell pepper, for Celia—and paella they'd just finished.

Everett had gone to the set with Park four days in a row, and he'd just finished explaining what he'd learned about the technical aspects of cinematography, how watching the camera operators would help his book, when Park picked up his guitar. He sat back from the table, the instrument in his lap, and picked at a flamenco melody. It sounded slower, less ornamented than what she typically associated with the style. He used the long nails of his fingers and thumbs to strum the strings, singly and in unison, and let the sound reverberate in the air for a moment before dampening it.

"He's been crazy for Spanish music ever since we saw that Woody Allen movie," Celia said.

"When I see something I like, I throw myself into it."

"I always wanted to learn guitar," Everett said. "Never had the discipline."

Rosalind looked at him, looking at Park. "I didn't know that."

"I thought you'd find it silly, me wanting to play an instrument."

Celia said, "Mom made me take piano as a kid, but sis always interrupted to correct me."

"I was trying to help."

"I couldn't go two pages without her butting in. She'd bump me off the bench and play it for me, hammering at the keys whenever she got to the places I messed up." Rosalind had heard her sister and Park arguing before dinner, though all she could make-out was Celia saying, *My brother-in-law*, twice. She feared that Park's patience with her tag-along of a husband had come to an end, but she didn't want to embarrass her sister, who refused to look at Park and addressed her comments to Everett instead, by bringing it up.

Rosalind said, "I thought we weren't talking about the past anymore."

"You feel like singing?" Park plucked the strings in thirds.

"I need more to drink first."

"She complains about not performing," Everett said, "but the music department wanted her to sing—what was it?"

"*Il Trovatore.* A recital, not the opera. Dr. Humphries is a fossil. No way he's accompanying me. God knows what he's teaching those poor singers."

"Catherine Marbaugh said she'd hire you if you got a master's."

"I don't need more schooling to be a better teacher than Humphries."

"I forgot how much fun listening to you two is" Celia said. "The Passive-Aggressive Olympics. If you're going to fight, fight."

Park played something faster, his fingers negotiating the strings while he looked toward the ocean. He had a clear, confident sound, attacking the notes so that even the mistakes sounded right, as though the composer were to blame. He hummed the harmony, making up syllables to go along with his playing, practically moaning. By the end, sweat glistened on his upper lip, and he wiped it away before finishing his wine and refilling everyone's glasses.

"How do you feel about subtitles?" He rested the guitar flat against his lap.

"People are too busy reading them to pay attention to the performance. How long would it take to learn about the opera beforehand—twenty minutes?"

Everett leaned forward, grasping his wine for support. "That's like saying you have to take batting practice before going to a baseball game."

"No, it isn't."

"She's right," Park said. "People should educate themselves. I wouldn't go to a baseball game without learning the rules and who's on the teams."

"What sports do they play in New Zealand?" Everett said.

"Way to stick to the topic, Doc," Celia said.

He shrugged. "What's wrong with wanting to learn about where you live?"

"My husband, the cultural ambassador." She picked up her glass. All of a sudden, she wanted to sing but felt embarrassed bringing it up.

"I'm serious." He sounded like their seven-year-old son.

"Nothing unusual. Cricket, rugby, golf, netball. Some sailing."

"What about surfing?"

"Not as much as here or Australia. But we know our way around a wave."

"I saw some boards in the garage."

"Are you saying you want to learn?" Celia said.

"Seems like fun."

"You're not much of a swimmer." Rosalind couldn't help sounding like his mother.

Park said, "We'll get up early, do it before we head to the set."

"I thought you were going to work on your book." Now she really felt like a scold.

"The pirates are going to board a merchant ship tomorrow. Park thinks it'll be choice."

"No worries," Park said. "I don't want to keep you from your work."

"I want to go," he said.

"You haven't even unpacked your books," Rosalind said.

"I'm letting my ideas breathe."

"Forget about them," Celia said. "I thought we would drive up the coast, see the Hearst Castle and spend some of that Hollywood money."

"You won't have to hear him complain when we get home and he hasn't gotten anything done."

"We're on vacation," Everett said.

"Lighten up, sis. He's a big boy."

Park retuned his guitar. "Rack off, both of you." He turned to her. "Let's shut them up."

He played a transposition of the flute arpeggios that open "Caro Nome," from *Rigoletto*, then repeated them when she didn't join him.

She watched his fingers move up and down the strings. "I haven't warmed up."

"We aren't expecting Carnegie Hall," Celia said.

"Take your time. I'll noodle around." He embellished on the intro but stuck close to Verdi's lines, went back to the original when she inhaled deeply.

She sat forward in her chair, back straight and feet planted for support, and began to sing. *Caro nome*— Sweet name. When she'd explained the opera to Everett years earlier, he'd compared this aria to Juliet's soliloquy early in Shakespeare's play, an apt analogy. Her voice was thin, unpracticed, and she had to concentrate to remember the libretto—she'd had more to drink than she thought—to hit the intervals midway through, but, in her mind, all of this fit with the character's youth. She was twice as old as Gilda, long past the teen's feelings—*you who made my heart throb for the first time.*

Park had clearly rehearsed, playing his part as fluidly as he'd played everything else, maintaining eye contact to let her know that he would follow her lead. She had to reach for the last lines—*and my last breath will be yours, my beloved*—the ingénue's true soprano a little out of her range, except on her best days. She couldn't hold the last note as long as she would have liked, the quaver in her voice more uncontrolled than the trill she had aimed for.

"Fucking brilliant," Park said after a long pause.

"You covered the weak spots."

"Bullshit. I just kept out of your way."

"He's right, sis." Celia's eyes were glassy, from wine or emotion, she couldn't tell which. "That was amazing."

"I don't know why the Lyric hasn't asked you back. Somebody must feel threatened."

"It's all politics," she lied. She felt good. None of them knew a thing about opera, not even Park, no matter how much he blustered, but their admiration buoyed her. She wanted to sing more, but Park hadn't learned Gilda's other aria, and she didn't feel confident enough to sing *a cappella*.

She went inside and splashed water on her face. Singing always made her warm, even without the elaborate costuming of a full-scale production, and she felt self-conscious about it, up close, even amongst family. She admired those who could do it with more ease, like Natalie Dessay, who she'd known a little when they were both new to the city, though already on different trajectories. The Frenchwoman was so petite yet effortless when she sang, her body quiet no matter the demands of the piece. Rosalind felt like a weekend karaoke singer by comparison.

Park was in the kitchen when she left the bathroom, piling dishes into the dishwasher. The studio had supplied no stemware but cupboards full of plates and bowls, delicate silver-edged china. Celia had already dropped a place-setting's worth.

"I'm knackered," he said. "Keeping up with you took a toll."

"You were great." She walked up behind him, watched him arrange the pots in the dishwasher so gently they didn't make a sound, didn't rub against each other. His hair fell in his face as he bent over, blond curls dangling against his thick eyebrows.

When he straightened, she embraced him from behind, looked out the window to make sure her sister and husband weren't paying attention, and kissed his neck. She tasted the tang of his sweat, mixed with the bitterness of the saffron he'd used in the paella.

"Rosalind," he said.

She moved around him, her calves pressed against the open door of the dishwasher, and groped for his lips with her own, but he resisted, holding her shoulders to keep her at arm's length. His grip was firm, steady, the way he'd held his guitar.

"You're lovely, dear, but Marie and Everett..."

She smiled, trying to be seductive, but he pushed her away, gently.

"I'm going to the loo. Why don't you go outside?"

Instead, she poured a glass of water. But even after the second glass, she could still taste him. Celia and Everett sat silently, her sister looking out at the darkened water, her husband studying the empty plastic cup he held, crushed, between his hands.

The weather was colder the next morning, and she sat on the beach with a scarf around her throat, wrapped in an afghan she'd found in their closet. It looked handmade, a garish mix of red, orange, and yellow, not what she expected to find in a Hollywood beach house. She'd dragged an Adirondack down the boardwalk, head throbbing each time a leg caught in the gaps between boards. It creaked as she reached for her coffee. She'd lost her sunglasses, but the dawn sky was overcast.

Park and Everett, encased in royal blue wetsuits, bobbed on surfboards fifty yards from shore, waiting for the proper wave to carry them toward her. Everett didn't even like the ocean, and now he wanted to be a surfer. In her current state, she couldn't make sense of it.

Her sister's feet whispered against the boards. As a child, she had been a lumbering, stomping drama queen, but yoga and adulthood had made her graceful, fluid.

"I'm surprised you're awake," Celia said. A wool sweater hung halfway down her legs, covering the tank top and most of the leggings she'd worn for yoga.

"The jackhammer in my head took care of that."

"I brought you some water." Celia handed her a bottle, then opened a beach chair and sat down beside her. "You need to rehydrate."

"Why am I the only one suffering?"

Celia sipped from her mug, the tea bag's string blowing in the wind. "I stopped drinking two hours before you. Park's got alcohol in his DNA. I've never seen him lose control."

The men made an attempt at the next wave, Park weaving back and forth on it, coming to a stop ten yards from shore, Everett standing unsteadily for a few seconds before falling head-first into the water, his left leg wrapped around the board as the rest of him went under.

"My husband's going to drown."

"Park'll look after him."

"Does he know what he's doing?"

"They'll be okay."

Park paddled back out, held the other board steady while Everett climbed on, and then led them farther out. Rosalind squinted, saw her husband shake his wet hair, like a dog, and nod at something Park said. They sat upright on their boards, letting the waves lift them, set the two of them down again, talking all the while.

"I kissed Park."

"I know. Bitch."

She couldn't tell if Celia was angry or amused. "He told you?"

"I saw it coming."

They looked at the water, Rosalind avoiding her sister's face. The men let more waves pass. Everett kicked his legs up and down on either side of his board, constantly in motion, while Park sat upright, swaying from side to side with the water.

"Why are you so calm?" she said.

"You think you're the first person to try that? What's-her-name, who plays Rory's mother in the movie? She offered to blow him in her trailer. On the first day."

"That doesn't answer my question."

"I told you, I'm used to it. And I'm no saint, either. Besides, I'm not the one who should be worried."

"Some actress is going to jump Everett? I love him, but I don't see that happening."

"I don't mean an actress."

Everett yelled and she looked up. He'd finally caught a wave, was zigzagging toward shore. His arms flailed as he tried to stay upright. Park was behind him, cutting his board back and forth to keep from speeding up, to avoid ramming into Everett, who was moving so slowly she was surprised he didn't fall over from inertia.

"What are you saying?"

"When we met, Park was living with a man called Thomas. They'd been together two years."

"He's gay?"

"Does he seem gay? We don't label each other like that."

"My head hurts too much for this."

"Too bad."

Everett finally tipped over, the board shooting forward a few feet before the tow rope pulled it back. When he came up, he was laughing, spitting water. Park gave him a hand, patted him on the back until he finished coughing. "One more," Everett yelled toward her, as though she was his mother and had called him to dinner. She could see his wide grin without squinting.

"You used to be so together," Celia said.

She remained silent, couldn't think of what to say to her little sister.

"Have you even called your kids since you got here?"

"Everett has. They're with *his* parents."

"What's going on with you?"

The men went out even farther, abandoned their boards and swam, treading water, cavorting like seals in their neoprene skins. She thought about them together but couldn't see it. Her sister was overly suspicious. And she'd accused *her* of being the judgmental one.

"Are you going to say anything?"

"I don't feel well. Think I'll lie down."

"Ignore me if you want, but at some point, you'll have to figure out what you want."

Rosalind stood up, swayed back and forth as a head rush threw her off balance. Her equilibrium returned, and she looked out to sea. The men were a tangle of limbs, water splashing around them as one head, then the other, went under, popped back up.

"They're killing each other," she said. And for that moment, she believed that they were.

TEAM PLAYER

My brother lives deep in the woods off County Road 19. Half a mile from his place, I catch a glimpse of his latest sculpture in a break in the tree line. A tall, spindly construction of metal rods that sways in the breeze, it looks like an ill-conceived radio tower. The medical school in Jackson commissioned it for the lobby of their new administrative building, but I doubt Russ's piece will fit beneath a roof. It must be twenty-five feet tall.

The driveway, marked by a dented mailbox with a perpetually raised flag, is an uneven dirt trail that meanders through the woods for a hundred yards before emptying into a small clearing. Even without the ruts to slow me down, I wouldn't drive more than ten miles per hour owing to Russ's black lab, Ramona. She's the leader of a pack of dogs who roam the area oblivious to the sight or sound of traffic. I hit one, once, in the dark, a black-and-white pointer, and though it survived both the collision and the work of the tipsy all-night veterinarian, it has a pronounced limp and a hatred for my truck it's passed on to its compatriots.

In the clearing, a generator hums next to a decrepit station wagon Russ stripped for a piece he'd done for some city in the Rust Belt, I can never remember which one. He abandons more sculptures than he finishes, and the remnants of these orphans litter the yard like a post-apocalyptic obstacle course—a five-foot-tall obelisk here,

what looks like a mutated stegosaurus skeleton there—
that I navigate more slowly than the driveway. Even so, I
run over a pile of scrap metal lying in the tall grass. The
land is part of a prairie reclamation project, so Russ has
an excuse for not owning a lawnmower or tidying up the
landscaping. Actually, I'm not sure he's allowed to live
here, legally, but he has ever since his last boyfriend threw
him out more than three years earlier, spending the first
year in a trailer that he converted into a workshop after
he ordered a metal-and-glass modular home from
Vancouver that he and I put together. Even where he
lives, tucked among the trees, the sun's reflection off the
silver cube is blinding.

He stands on the scaffold near the top of the piece,
blow torch in one hand, three-foot-long wrought-iron
bar in the other. The sculpture consists of the fences that
used to surround four nearby family graveyards. I drove
him from location to location last May, where he haggled
with the families, none of whom bore any relation to the
names on the markers in their private cemeteries. Only
one couple, yuppies from up north who'd moved here to
get in touch with the land, caused a problem, but once
they learned that Russ wasn't some nut, that he had a
piece in the sculpture garden in their hometown, they
seemed honored he'd selected their scrap.

Sparks rain down from the scaffold, ticking against
the rusted metal on their way to the ground, where they
smolder, then burn out in the dirt. The sculpture is a
gigantic replica of a double-helix, each fence representing
one of the four bases. He claims to have modeled it on

Larry Bird's DNA, but when I asked him how he knew Bird's genetic code, he just stared at me.

He refuses to be interrupted while he's working—not in an arrogant way; more like he plain doesn't *see* anybody—so I wait for him to notice me, sitting on the hood of my Mid-South Food Group pick-up. Once he does, he works another fifteen minutes before swinging down from the scaffold like Tarzan descending a tree.

"What did I do this time?" he says, scratching his beard with a soot-covered hand. He has the thickest, blackest hair I've ever seen, on his head and face, arms and legs, back and chest. I'm five years younger, but my hair has begun to thin, leaving a tonsure on the crown of my head that seems to even the age gap.

"What's today?"

"Wednesday?"

I shake my head.

"You win. You're Captain Calendar. What's going on?"

"Your class? Why didn't Victoria pick you up?" Russ never learned to drive—rather, he never learned to pass the driving exam—so his assistant, or I, chauffeur him everywhere.

"She doesn't work for me anymore."

"That's what I heard." Russ teaches one studio course per semester at Magnolia, for which he's paid like a full professor, so when he doesn't show, which happens a few times each semester, the secretary calls me, as though I don't have a job of my own to do. This time, however, Dr. Drury, the Chair, called himself. "Tell your brother nobody's untouchable as long as the economy's this bad," he said. Not that I'll ever give Russ that message.

"So why bother asking?" He roams the yard looking for one of the basketballs he keeps handy. Once he finds one, he squeezes it, frowns, then moves toward the hoop attached to the side of the trailer.

"She lasted longer than the others," I say. "You should buy her a gold watch."

He backs an imaginary opponent toward the basket, spins right, and banks in a hook shot. The ball bounces back to him, and he slings it at me without looking. "I asked her to find a model for a piece I want to do, and she must have thought I was too shy to ask her directly, so she volunteered."

"She thought you were *shy?*"

"If you're not going to shoot, hand it over."

I pass him the ball, knowing that if I miss the basket, he'll stop his story to explain what I've done wrong and make me take the shot again.

"Her proportions are all wrong. I could tell I'd hurt her feelings, so I explained that her hips and ass are too wide for the metal I want to use."

"Her hips look okay to me." She and I spent a day together, putting up the scaffolding for the med school statue. Though I'm sure that afternoon has blurred with all the other grunt work she did for Russ, I still remember the dotting of freckles on her pale shoulders, peeking out from the straps of her tank top, the slight curve of her stomach against the waistband of her khaki shorts.

"Jesus, Cal. She's twenty." Easy for him to say. He could have his pick of coeds, male or female.

"It's an aesthetic judgment."

"Leave those to me." Russ dribbles into the post again, makes the same spin move, except to the left, and shoots with his off-hand, the ball going up softer this time, rolling halfway around the rim before dropping in. As a kid, he practiced moves like this for hours, alternating between his right and left hands, though he never had any interest in joining a team. "If she's going to be an artist, she's going to need a better eye, and more confidence."

He jogs away from the basket, misses a twenty-foot jump shot, and lets the ball roll toward the trees, where one of the dogs will no doubt get a hold of it. He loses a dozen a year this way.

"It's coming along." I'm not supposed to mention his work—he likes to pretend it doesn't exist in any identifiable form until he's finished, as though it emerges whole, like that goddess who popped out of Zeus's head—but I can't help it this time. "Kind of big, isn't it?"

"That's the point."

"Didn't they give you dimensions?"

"Aren't you supposed to be at work?"

"Exactly. But when you skip class and won't answer your phone, who do you think they try next? And in case you're wondering, I don't have time to find you a new assistant."

"Call the secretary." He looks up at the sculpture, its shadow falling over us in warped Xs. "I'm too busy to teach, anyway."

"That's not the attitude they're looking for."

He walks away, toward the trailer's front door. "They didn't hire me for my teaching. They hired me for my genius." He says *genius* without any irony or sarcasm, the way he did when we were kids and he aced the IQ test in *Boys' Life*.

*

I spend most of the next twenty-four hours at the football stadium, buried amid sleeves of souvenir cups and 250-count bundles of hot dog wrappers. I'm the manager of concessions for all university sporting events, and I only have two days to inventory and distribute one-hundred-thousand dollars' worth of merchandise before Saturday's game. With the football team tanking, attendance has been poor, so my sales have been down as well, which led the higher-ups in Memphis to lay off most of my warehouse workers, as though overstaffing and not the losing streak caused the dip. By six on Friday, I've done everything I can until the vendors arrive before the game, which eliminates my excuse for skipping dinner with my parents.

My mother meets me at the door, an empty martini glass dangling by its stem between the thumb and forefinger of her left hand. She smiles more broadly than usual and hugs me tightly with her free arm.

"You didn't tell me there would be company." In the driveway, I parked behind one of my father's construction pick-ups and an unfamiliar SUV.

"Your father invited a few people. Oh, sweetheart, you stink."

"I've been at the stadium all day."

"Well…" She holds me at arm's length. "You don't have time for a shower, but at least change shirts. You've got mustard all over this one." She opens the hall closet and pulls out a plaid shirt—*plaid* plaid, the kind a five-year-old would wear in a family Christmas card photo—that still has a price tag poking through one of the buttonholes. "I saw this at Heppners' and thought it would be perfect for you."

"You haven't bought me clothes in ten years. So help me, if you're trying to fix me up again, I'm leaving. How many times do I have to tell you I'm too busy for a girlfriend?" I promised myself I'd lose twenty pounds before I dove into the dating pool again—my last relationship fizzled out when Becca moved eleven hundred miles away to study Chinese medicine. I hadn't known she had any interest in it, let alone that she was contemplating leaving, until a week before her lease was up and she took off. Sucker that I am, I still helped her load the U-Haul.

"Nothing like that," she says, heading for the kitchen. "Hurry up and get changed. We're having your favorite."

Even DeNiece and Rhonda, my mother's kitchen help, can't keep from smiling when they see me in my new shirt. I'm a big guy, and a huge swath of brown-and-red plaid does nothing to mask this. It makes me look like a walking tablecloth.

A few years ago, flush with money from their expanding construction business, my parents tore down the ranch house Russ and I grew up in, and our neighbor's identical one once they'd purchased it, and replaced these with an enormous, Spanish-style villa, complete with a colonnaded gallery, a Mediterranean courtyard, and a fountain shipped all the way from Seville. The courtyard, a *casas-patio*, is where I find my parents and their guests once I've sampled the shrimp grits and opened a beer. They've turned off the fountain again—bullfrogs keep getting stuck in the drain and drowning—so I can hear my shoes squeak against the marble floor beneath the colonnade.

My father stands at the outdoor bar, pouring martinis, his right-hand man, Terry, stationed beside him. He's worked for my father for twenty-five years, and this is maybe the fifth time I've seen him in a pressed shirt. He's buttoned the blue, long-sleeved Oxford all the way to the top, where his Adam's apple looks crushed between loose flesh and the shirt's starched collar. He nods, once, when he sees me before turning away. As far as I can tell, my father is the only person other than his sister he even remotely likes.

"I thought I was going to have to send Terry to drag you out of the kitchen," my father says when he sees me.

"I know how much you like DeNiece's grits." He smiles a big, toothy grin, like my mother's, and steers me towards his guests.

"This is my boy, Calvin," he says, introducing me to Horace and Shirley Keogh.

"Of course it is." Mr. Keogh stands up to shake my hand, beaming as he does so.

With all this cheery goodwill, I feel like the guest of honor at a Rotary dinner. "How do y'all know each other?"

My father smiles even more broadly and puts his arm around me, a sign not of affection but of his desire for me to shut up. "Mr. Keogh and I are doing some business together, but we can talk about that later." He winks at Mrs. Keogh and picks up the cigar resting in a glass ashtray on the coffee table. He keeps the local tobacco shop in business, smoking upwards of ten Dominicans a week in place of the four-to-a-pack stink sticks he used to buy at a gas station and parcel out like they were gold.

The Keoghs are older than my parents, mid-seventies, I would guess, and keep their hands in their laps, drinks clutched close to them so they don't spill, and look around like tourists at Graceland. From his calloused hands and thick fingernails, I figure Mr. Keogh is a farmer whose land my father wants to buy, which is borne out by how overly-solicitous my parents are. Even Terry gets into the act, refilling their glasses with iced tea when they run low. The Keoghs share a look each time my father heads to the bar for the other refills.

"Calvin," my mother says, "will you escort Mrs. Keogh to the dinner table?"

I offer the woman my arm, but she pops up from the chaise on her own, looking spryer and stronger than me, and it's all I can do to keep up with her on our way inside. As we pass through the kitchen, she gawks at the two middle-aged women in black-and-white livery. I'd do the same if I didn't feel so bad for the ladies right now.

Rhonda has set the table with the best china, silver, and crystal. Platters of shrimp grits, fried okra, and corn bread sit on the side board, next to a decanter of red wine. Once we're seated and my father has said the blessing, something he hasn't done since I was confirmed in eighth grade, when he decided he'd done his duty by my immortal soul, Mr. Keogh turns to me and says, "It sure is a pleasure meeting you. The missus and I go to every game."

My mother, sitting on my left, rests her hand on my arm, and I look past her to my father at the head of the table. Mr. Keogh goes on undeterred.

"When y'all beat Miami that year, I told everyone you'd go undefeated, but nobody believed me. After the Georgia game, folks were talking like they'd knowed it all along."

"The Keoghs have had season tickets every year since—when was it Horace?"

"1970. The year before they let those black boys on the team."

"I'll be," my father says. "I hope I'm not embarrassing you, Horace, but I think Calvin should

211

know that when I asked you to dinner, the first thing you said was, 'Will your son be there?'"

"You have another son, don't you," Mrs. Keogh asks my mother.

My father responds before she can open her mouth, feigning nonchalance. "He's an *artiste*. Too good for his old parents, isn't that right?"

"If that's what you think," I say.

Mr. Keogh taps me on the arm, cautiously, the way kids still do at the stadium. "That catch you made was the prettiest thing I've ever seen."

"The Orange Bowl," my father says. "Tell him, Cal. I'm sure the Keoghs would enjoy hearing it from your perspective."

I wipe my mouth on the linen napkin. "You're the storyteller."

"Any chance to brag on his son," my mother says, patting my hand one more time before letting go.

My father pushes his plate away from him so he can lean forward, elbows braced against the table to keep him from getting too agitated. "Down by four with fifteen seconds left," he says—though, if you want to get specific about it, there were only twelve— "and the ball's on the twenty-one yard line. They're out of time-outs, so this is it. Brewster drops back—hell of quarterback, isn't he, Horace? You see that game he had against the Bengals last week?"

Before Mr. Keogh can answer, my father waves him away. "Ohio State sends five guys at him—I never

212

understood why their coach did that with y'all in the spread. What do you think?"

"Maybe he was drunk," I say.

My father laughs, slaps the table like what I've said is the funniest damn thing he's ever heard. "Brewster roles out of the pocket, cause if there's one thing we couldn't do right that year—and I mean *only* one thing—it was protecting the quarterback. But since they rushed so many, it was one-on-one downfield, and our boy here—" he looks to my mother, graciously including her in their parental success story—"sees a seam in the defense and goes deeper than he's supposed to. Probably gave Coach Vernon a heart attack. He's standing on the two when Brewster looks his way. And Calvin, who probably dropped as many passes as he caught that year—no offense, son, but it's true—jumps higher than I've ever seen him and hangs onto that ball with the tippiest tops of his fingertips, even after that safety walloped him, and scores. Game over. Hello, national championship!"

"We tied for the championship, remember?"

"The coaches poll voted y'all number one," Mr. Keogh says. "That's who I trust, not a bunch of Yankee writers." We sit in silence, savoring the moment, and then Mr. Keogh adds, "I never understood why that other boy complained about your catch. The important thing is y'all won the game."

"That's right," my father says. He looks at me. "Some people just aren't team players."

In the excitement after the game, no one thought to wonder why a tight end with hands of stone—my father was right about my knack for dropping balls—was twenty yards beyond the line of scrimmage, that is until Willie Nix, our best wide receiver and the *boy* Mr. Keogh referred to, mentioned it to a reporter in the locker room while the rest of us danced around singing "We Are the Champions." When I caught the ball, Willie was standing behind me in the end zone, a step ahead of his defender, where he could have made a much easier, though less dramatic, catch. The coaches sat on him as soon as they realized how much better the story sounded the way folks like my father tell it. Within a few days, when the occasional sports-radio or TV commentator took Willie's side, they were shouted down for being naysayers. I haven't seen Willie in years; last I heard, he was returning punts for a team in Canada.

The good feeling spreads so far around the table that even my mother, who hates football, joins in. "You should have seen your father, yelling so hard his face turned red. He ended up hyperventilating. Everyone around us was dancing, bumping into each other, and I told him, 'if you don't calm down, you're going to blow a gasket, and the paramedics will never get through this crowd in time to save you.'"

"Hell, Lizzie, Doc Adderley was two rows behind us singing 'Hail to the Chiefs' with the rest of us."

"Sure, but he'd had even more to drink than you had."

As I said, we won a share of the National Championship, for the first time in sixty-odd years, but nobody made as much of our success as my father. At the time, he was building cheap duplexes and student rentals. Once I'd made the most memorable play in school history, he co-opted the image for the print and television ads that touted his new stretch of Game Day Condos, elegant townhouses within walking distance of the stadium that he sold to football-obsessed alums beginning the following season, while school spirit remained at its peak. With those profits, he bought up pastures and fields and built small, cookie cutter houses and a separate high-end subdivision of four- and five-bedroom homes. By the time the football team had slid back into mediocrity three years later, he'd become the biggest land owner around here since Reconstruction.

After Terry and the Keoghs leave, my father takes me into his study, where he shows me the plans for what he wants to do with their land. "According to that guy who writes for the *Commercial Appeal*, the condo bubble's going to bust any day now, so I'm going to *diversify*—" he pauses on the word as though it's a concept he's invented—"build a fancy apartment complex. Tennis courts, pool and gym, the works. Hell, if the Keoghs can get their neighbors to sell, I might even put in a golf course."

"Sounds pricy."

"Folks want amenities these days without the hassle of the upkeep. Maybe you'll finally work for me, manage the place."

"Will the Keoghs sell?"

He leans back in the leather captain's chair. "You saw how old they are. I don't imagine they'll want to work that farm much longer. You could have helped out a little, you know. Been more enthusiastic."

"You could have warned me what I was getting into."

"And risk you not showing up? No, thank you."

We sit in silence for a few minutes, my father pouring over the future of his empire while I study the framed map on the wall behind his desk. He's taken to collecting historical artifacts—an ashtray used by Clement Attlee at Potsdam, Patton's binoculars from the invasion of Sicily. The map on the wall is of Omaha Beach, from General Bradley's headquarters on the *Augusta.*

Finally, my father rolls up his plans, places them back in their cardboard tube, and turns to me. "Terry and I went by your house. You need to cut the grass. It's awfully shaggy."

My father gave me one of his cheapie, two-bedroom houses when I graduated from Magnolia. Of the thirty-two identical homes, mine is the only one he was unable to sell, because it sits by a road the high-school kids drag race down and overlooks the state highway off-ramp. It took me six years to graduate—including two years plus summer school, post-Orange Bowl, to make up for my bare minimum course loads during football—but I'm the first in my family to finish college, Russ having dropped out of SCAD his junior year when he got into the Whitney Biennial. It kills my father that, four years later, I still refuse his show of appreciation.

"You know I don't want it."

"Fine," he says, exhaling cigar smoke. "Then rent the damn thing out, I don't care. Just do *something* with it. I don't understand why you pay rent when you've got a house, free-and-clear, you could be living in."

"What if I want it to sit empty with the lawn turning to seed?"

He closes one eye and glares at me with the other, the way he used to when I was a kid and gave my mother a hard time at the dinner table. "No wonder you've got such a lousy job. No ambition. No... *imagination*."

*

The next day, Magnolia gives up seventeen points in the first quarter, and by halftime, people are fleeing the stadium. The sky has opened into a downpour, so the remaining fans, the loyalists, the drunks, and those with nothing better to do, crowd the mezzanines and covered ramps, making it difficult for me to maneuver a cart of bagged ice and bottled water from stand to stand on level C. My left ankle acts up whenever it rains—no matter how much I taped it in college, it tended to roll, so I spent more of my playing days with it sprained than healthy— which only adds to the fun of restocking inventory among a sea of distraught people.

"Hey," somebody yells as I pass by. "I know you."

I keep going, looking straight ahead. I'm hungry and tired. I don't need this.

The man catches up to me, and I can see out of the corner of my eye that he's staring. He watches me so intently that he plows through a family of five like they're bowling pins, knocking over a young boy, and jostles a pack of sorority girls, dressed to the nines, as is undergrad custom at games.

"You're Calvin Hodges." He trots ahead of me to get a better look, then mimics my catch. "I was supposed to go to that game, but my wife went into labor. You believe that luck?"

I clip someone's heel with the cart, shout, "coming through," and try to get around my fan. I didn't used to be this way, but it gets to you, always being reminded of the past.

"Shit, man. That was incredible." Even up close, he has to yell for his voice to carry above the din echoing off the concrete walls of the mezzanine. Every time he opens his mouth, I smell bourbon. "I can't believe I missed that game."

We stop at a stand, where I heft bags of ice over the counter to the troop leader supervising his uniformed Cub Scouts. I tell him I'll be back for the halftime deposit once the third quarter starts, but he tells me it isn't worth the trip. During slow games like this one, I usually stay at each stand for a few minutes, shooting the breeze with the workers, but today I only want to keep moving, get back to the windowless room where the two ladies from the bank keep track of the deposits.

All along, my new best friend waits, hopping from foot to foot like a kid in need of a bathroom. Magnolia's a dry campus but try telling that to folks on game days. The university even provides courtesy lockers outside the skyboxes and University Club for the High Rollers, as my father calls them. They come in during the week to lay in provisions before security covers the gates to search for bottles and flasks. Everyone else has to be creative.

"Can you believe we're losing to Western Kentucky? I mean, shit, did *you* ever lose to them? I bet they didn't get within two touchdowns of y'all."

I tell him I didn't have much to do with the outcome, either way.

"Like hell." He mimes the catch again, half-heartedly this time, beginning to run out of steam. It isn't easy maintaining excitement in the face of such a killjoy. "Can I have an autograph?"

He hands me this year's team guide, where my picture is on page forty-one, in the Great Moments in Chiefs History section. It's black-and-white this time, a little smaller than last year's quarter-page layout, but it still brings everything back. I've heard that in big moments like this, time is supposed to slow down, but the opposite happened for me. I saw the ball leave the quarterback's hand, and before I had time to register where it was headed, or worry about dropping it, it was tucked against my chest and I was bracing for the hit that sent me sprawling into the end zone.

I have trouble holding the pen on account of the syrup coating my fingers from a leaky bag-in-a-box of Pepsi, but I do my best to sign my name and number, 85, though it feels foolish after so many years. How many 85s have come and gone since me?

"That's awesome," the man says when I hand him the guide, studying the signature as though I'm a big deal. We shake hands before going our separate ways, him to his seat, me back to work.

I don't mean to sound ungrateful for the attention, but this guy, my father, Mr. Keogh, everybody except Willie Nix, has the wrong idea about what happened. In reality, I made as many mistakes as possible on the play. I'd been penalized twice for false starts in the second half, so I reacted slowly to the snap, not wanting to jump early and cost us five more yards. When I did begin my route, a linebacker, one of those blitzers my father talked about, knocked me so off course that I ended up seven yards deeper than I should have been, which explains why I was even in Willie's vicinity. The image everyone remembers from the game, which made the cover of the leading sports magazines and the following year's team guide, not to mention my father's billboards, was a one-in-a-million for a guy like me, as opposed to the routine play it would have been for Willie. The strong safety who blind-sided me gave me a concussion, and my falling into the end zone instead of back onto the playing field was sheer providence, as the migraines that have plagued me ever since never fail to remind me.

*

After the game, it takes me forty minutes to fight through the traffic around the square and the pedestrians, drunk on liquor and disappointment, milling in the streets. The university's student body equals the town's population, but on game weekends the visitors outnumber both groups combined. If not for the money I have to put in the night deposit, I would give up and walk home from the stadium. I could use the exercise. I rent a carriage house from a lawyer-couple who live in the three-story Victorian that looms over my place, filling a double lot a few blocks off the square. When I turn off the alley and into my narrow parking space, I see all the lights blazing, the curtains open. I sit in the truck for a moment, the thump of a bass guitar audible from one of the bars on the square, and watch my brother. He looks like an adult in a kids' play house, the way he's framed in the narrow window. He stands at the stove, stirring a pot with a wooden spoon. He's got a tumbler of scotch in his hand from a bottle that costs more than I made today. The liquor store has to special order it. The owner calls me whenever he gets a new bottle.

Inside, I can smell the chili on the stovetop. Russ refuses to buy a television, so he hitches a ride into town on Saturdays to watch the games at my place. I've offered to get him tickets, but he hates crowds. He has on a gray t-shirt that shows off the muscles he's acquired from years of sculpting and a pair of jeans that are too short on account of how frayed the bottoms have become. His arms are pink from the abrasive soap he uses to scrub the soot and debris.

"That coach should have to pay us for wasting time on that game," he says. "Maybe I'll start a class-action suit."

I'm too tired to play along, so I only nod. "That smells good."

"It's almost ready."

Something about the way he says this forces the tumblers in my mind into place: he's cleaned himself up, he's cooking, he's taken down my world atlas and left it open on the two-seat kitchen table.

"You finished," I say.

"Thirty hours straight. I only stopped to piss and feed the dogs." He tastes the chili, then adds, "It's a piece of shit."

"You always say that."

"Maybe they're all shit." He adds more black pepper to the pot. "Get cleaned up. You stink."

"That's the second time this week someone's told me that. I'm starting to take offense."

My father is right about my place being small, but I like it that way. A house, even one as simple as the two-bedroom he gave me, has more space than I know what to do with. And, illogical as it sounds, I saw what happened to my parents when they upgraded. I prefer my tiny living room, which Russ and I fill. We sit on opposite ends of my couch, staring in the direction of the muted television in the corner, taking turns walking the nine steps to the kitchen for more beer and scotch and to refill our bowls. Chili is one of the few dishes my brother knows how to cook. He adds black olives, green peppers, and celery to the tomato and onion base, and holds back the ground veal, the finest cut he can find, until the last possible second. In the kitchen, he's either an idiot or a gourmand. He can't figure out how to tell when pasta is ready, but he can make a lamb roast so good I'd choose it for my last supper. His chili is just what I need after a day of catch-as-catch-can eating—a hot dog at eleven and another at 5:30, popcorn and M&Ms seeing me through the rest of the way. Vintage Russ. After months of selfishness and unreliability, he offers this unexpected gift. Our parents, who he hasn't spoken to in so long it no longer seems out of the ordinary, don't understand this. Being self-absorbed themselves, they view the same trait in their eldest as some kind of betrayal without realizing that his attention in moments like this makes up for all the grocery shopping, bill paying, and personal assistant-monitoring I do for him.

He tells me about his plan to go to Italy—he claims there are hardly any tourists this time of year—the museums and architecture he wants to see, the unknown *trattoria* a friend-of-a-friend owns in Naples. "Why don't you come with me?" he says.

"I can't take vacation during the school year."

"So quit. There are plenty of better jobs."

"You sound like Dad." If not for the five beers I've finished, I would never say this, even though it is true in so many ways.

"Then I take it back. You should stay here and let that job rot your brain until people standing next to you can smell the stench coming out of your ears."

I stretch out my legs, resting them on the coffee table. The morning after games, I can hardly bend my knees, on account of spending twelve hours standing on concrete. I feel them stiffening already. "Sure. I'll go off with you, then come back and choose from the long list of exciting, rewarding jobs people are *dying* to offer me." After a moment, I add, "Why is it that everyone else knows exactly what I should be doing with my life?"

He shakes his head, disappointed. Russ likes to plan expensive, elaborate trips after he finishes a piece—he's hiked the Andes and the Urals, walked miles of the Great Wall of China, and eaten his way through North Africa—but he always abandons them halfway through, when a new project comes to mind, as it did, twice, while we were building his house. Four months went by when only the external walls and roof were in place. In the end, we completed three-quarters of it in a two-week period when he couldn't figure out how to finish Sisyphus in Hades. As soon as he made his breakthrough—he wrapped Sisyphus in steel mesh to contrast with his cast iron underworld—he left me to install the fixtures while he worked around the clock for five days. A wealthy broker in Dallas bought the piece and donated it to a museum in Fort Worth, where it sits, as Russ likes to point out, near a Twombly and a Kiefer. More than two years old now, it's still his most recent major work.

✣

As always, Dave, my boss, arrives late for our monthly meeting, which gives me time to finish the paperwork from the weekend. My office was the kitchen in the athletes' dormitory until the NCAA cracked down on that type of student segregation. The work space consists of all the counters, range tops, walk-in freezers, and ovens necessary to feed four-story's worth of two-hundred-fifty-pound Neanderthals. The far corner holds a scarred desk with one leg half an inch shorter than the others, a five-year-old computer, and a dented filing cabinet. The fluorescent bulbs flicker and hum overhead, exacerbating my all-too-frequent headaches. And Memphis wonders why we never turn a decent profit.

The outer door at the far end of the kitchen bangs open at 11:30, thirty minutes late. "You in here, Cal?"

"In the back."

Dave mutters to himself, keys jangling at his side, comes around the corner, and crashes into the filing cabinet, knocking a stack of unprocessed sky box catering orders onto the floor. "You should lay down bread crumbs or give out a map or something," he says, thrusting his hand forward. He is a slight man, only a few years older than me, though he's gone completely gray. In a double-breasted suit with lapels as wide as his shoulders, he looks like a kid dressing up as a 1930s gangster.

We eat at a diner north of town, the same place we go every time he comes to check on me, the same place where my father and Terry eat lunch. Dave orders a turkey sandwich, like he always does, and the waitress gives him a look, knowing that he could get a better deli sandwich at any number of restaurants on the square. He prefers to eat here, however, for the same reason my father does: it makes them feel like common men, not upper management.

"Your operation isn't exactly a cash cow." He crams part of his sandwich into his mouth, bites it in half, and sets what's left on his plate, saliva glistening on the crust of the toasted white bread. He eats like a kid, biting off more than he can chew, his eyes bulging while his jaws work over the ball of food in his mouth.

"It's been a tough season."

"So was the last one, and the one before that."

"Our numbers have held steady. They're better than when I took over."

"I'm not saying it's your fault." He frowns, working on a recalcitrant bite, then picks at the gap between his front teeth. "We've decided not to put in a bid after this year."

"You're pulling out?"

"This place has never performed the way we wanted it to. I don't want to think about how bad it would be if you weren't here killing yourself for us." He leans forward, the buttons on his suit coat ticking against the Formica tabletop. "Things are almost as bad in Nashville, but we're locked in for another three years, so that's where we're putting our energies. Kenny's a good guy, but he's in over his head. I'm hoping you'll go up there and help him out, watch over things for us."

"Is that a demotion?"

"More like when a team takes a coach, a *successful* coach, and gives him a job as an advisor. It's less responsibility and structure, but that doesn't mean it isn't important."

My whole life, teachers and bosses have used sports analogies to explain things to me, as though I can't understand anything else. "Sounds like you're putting me out to pasture."

"I shouldn't tell you this, but we're going after the Titans contract in another year, and when we get it, I want to put you in charge. If you go along with me on this Vandy deal, it'll show everyone what a team player you are."

"Don't you mean *if* you get the contract?"

A shadow falls over our table, and I look up to see my father, with Terry behind him, a green baseball cap cocked back on his head so that the underside of the bill obscures the logo.

"I was just saying I needed to call you, and here you are." He has that glow he gets whenever he's been out surveying his empire. "I got an interesting call from Horace Keogh this morning. Turns out he's decided not to sell, but—" my father turns to Terry as he says this— "he *promises* that when he's ready to, he'll let me know."

"Dad, this is Dave Fowler, my boss. He came down from Memphis."

"Yes," Dave says, rising to shake hands. "I'm here to talk about Cal's future."

"I hope you're having more luck with this boy than I have. He tell you about his sales pitch the other night?"

227

"At the Western Kentucky game?" Flustered, Dave pumps Terry's hand once and returns to his seat.

My father smirks. "Didn't we lose that game by about *fifty* points," he says, as though soggy hotdogs and watered-down drinks have something to do with the score. He pats me on the back a little too hard, then heads for the booth across the aisle. Before he sits down, he calls out, "Valerie, honey, put my boy's lunch on my tab." He and Terry don't bother looking at the menus. Instead, he calls out their orders without consulting his co-worker. Then he leans toward me and says, "You need to work on your people skills. I had Keogh set up. All I needed was for you to charm him a little. Think about your brother. He could have had old Horace's pants around his ankles within ten minutes."

Dave smiles uncomfortably, looking from me to my father and back again.

"You've got it wrong, Dad. With a mouth like that, you're the real charmer in the family."

I get up to leave, Dave trailing behind me, and put a twenty on the front counter. I'll be damned if my father's paying for this meal.

At the door, Dave points to the framed photograph of me making the catch above the register and says, "What a shame." A spidery crack spreads from the lower right-hand corner of the glass, as though someone tried to put an elbow through it.

*

228

By Friday the weather has turned blustery, dead leaves rattling in the trees. It's a light week—men's and women's soccer, an invitational tennis tournament—so I try to regroup. Even if I can't keep this branch going, I need to do something. I process the outstanding orders, send the last month's financial statements to Memphis a week early, and complete the inventory in preparation for next Saturday's football game. I even clean the office, pulling out the kitchen equipment to mop the floors from wall to wall, and have my truck washed and waxed. None of this will make a difference, I know, but keeping busy feels good, distracts me from Dave's offer. I work so hard I'm able to take a half-day on Friday to make it to Russ's for The Powers That Be's first look at his finished product.

Russ is describing his process to a group of four— the Dean of the Medical School, two members of its Board of Directors, and their leading donor—when I arrive. He explains the decision to focus on a DNA strand as the fundamental connection between all the fields of medicine, the hours he and I spent searching for the appropriate materials, and his technique, which incorporated those of the time periods when the various fences had originally been constructed with more recent methods that will insure its longevity.

When he finishes, the four walk around the piece, striking the universal Looking-at-Art pose: arms folded across their chests, heads cocked like Ramona when she hears an unfamiliar command. Finally, Dr. Wall, the donor, says, "Is it just me or does it seem a little *rusted?*"

He glances at the others for confirmation, sheepish for having raised such a qualm.

"I took the oxidization process into consideration when I began. I suppose I could have scrubbed all the pieces clean, but I prefer this. I find the lack of uniformity appealing."

Wall nods eagerly. "Still, it looks a little *flimsy*."

"How closely have you looked at a DNA molecule. I mean—" Russ stops and turns toward the other three, who talk among themselves. "I'm sorry. I didn't catch that."

"Stay calm," I whisper to him, but he ignores me. This happens all the time. Russ never travels the easy road, never does what anyone expects, and it often takes critics, gallery owners, and buyers some time to adjust their expectations.

He shakes his head at me, then walks closer to the others.

"We were discussing the fact that this is too big," the Dean says. "It's easily a story too tall."

I hate that I mentioned the size the other week, but Russ doesn't even look at me, he's so focused on the others. When it comes to his work, he holds a *you're either with me or against me* attitude, leaving no room for fence-sitters.

He shrugs. "It would look better outdoors," he says.

The female board member steps forward. "We hired you to build something for our atrium."

"You didn't hire me—I'm not a carpenter. You *commissioned* me to create something that will grab people's attention and serve as a goddamn monument to what goes on in your school. That's what this is. It's not my problem where you put it."

"Commissioned, hired, it doesn't change the fact that we gave you money with certain restrictions in mind. This..." She looks up, fortifying herself with another glance at the offending piece. "This does not *come close* to meeting them."

The Dean says, "Maybe if you trimmed it a little?"

"It's not a fucking haircut." Russ walks away, toward the trailer, and I follow, catching a glimpse of Ramona and her pack as they scurry around the workshop's corner and out of sight. Russ kicks an empty acetylene tank aside and sits down on the steps, his clenched fists resting on his knees.

"They'll get used to it," I say.

"*Trimmed it?* I'd rather give them back the fucking money." His jaw is set when he looks up at me, his gaze focused over my shoulder, at the quartet gathered near the sedan with the medical school seal embossed on the driver's side door. Anyone else would see defiance in this look, but I know him well enough to notice the panic beneath the surface. He reminds me of a cat we used to have, Apples, who would climb the tallest trees in our yard, then hunker near the top, yowling until our father got a ladder off one of his trucks and went after her. He'd come down cursing while she screeched and clawed at his shirt, arms, and face. As soon as they were within a few feet of the ground, she'd launch herself away from him and run off, our father giving chasing, kicking at the darting creature.

"That's what you want?"

He nods. "If I could."

"They're ready to go."

"You deal with them. I'm going inside."

As I walk toward the group, I notice one of Russ's failures, a birdcage-like dome made out of rebar and old railroad spikes. It was the first thing he worked on after he moved out here, and grass and weeds have grown up around it, a sticker bush blooming inside, trapped like an exhibit in a zoo.

I feel like I did during parent-teacher conferences when I was a kid, except that back then I had to sit in a chair in the hallway, straining to make out the mumbling I heard on the other side of the classroom door while now I'm the one on the inside. "I'm sure we can work something out," I say, not positive even I believe it this time. "Russ is passionate about his ideas, but I know he wants you to be happy with his work."

The woman stands by the sedan's passenger side door, about to get in. She stops to look at me, studying the Mid-South logo on my polo shirt, the dried popcorn oil stain on my right breast that had dribbled down the front like blood from a gunshot wound. "That isn't the impression I got," she says.

"He has a strong vision. That's how he's made it this far."

The Dean comes around from the driver's side and says, "I'm sorry, who are you?"

"I'm his brother."

"Do you have authority to speak for him?"

"I do right now."

"Then tell him we expect the changes we discussed. Otherwise—"

"I don't remember much discussion. I heard you telling him what to do, and him explaining why he can't do that. We're willing to discuss a compromise, but it can't be one-sided."

"This is a waste of my time," Dr. Wall says. He looks to the Dean. "I never understood why we needed a sculpture in the first place."

The Dean's face reddens as he opens the back door for the older man.

"Excuse me for a second," I say before he can get into the car. It takes effort for me to keep my voice steady. "If you can't see what a masterpiece this is, what an impact it could have for your school, then we *should* give you back the money. I'm sure someone else would be happy to buy it."

Wall doesn't even blink, though I take his unwillingness to make eye contact as a minor victory. "It looks like an enormous heap of scrap to me. If someone else feels differently, by all means try to convince them otherwise."

✻

233

When I tell my father I'm putting my house on the market, he's happier than I've seen him since the Orange Bowl, assuming I've found a good use for the money, but once he learns the truth, he refuses to speak to me. In the three months it takes to find a buyer willing to pay the asking price, I see my father and Terry driving around town occasionally, at the diner on the day I give Dave my two weeks' notice, and one-on-one at home both times I try to patch up our differences. He refuses to acknowledge me on these occasions, let alone listen to my side of the story, and once I've given up trying, I realize his disappointment doesn't bother me.

My last day working for Mid-South, I pay all of my remaining employees' overtime to help me move from the carriage house into Russ's second bedroom. Dave would consider this gross mismanagement. Even if he finds out, it won't matter. My new employer doesn't care about trivial details like this. He's in Italy, on an open-ended ticket, recuperating from the trauma of *Double-Helix, 33* and its aftermath—the medical school board filed papers for breach of contract two weeks before my house cleared escrow, and Russ had to add the bulk of his savings to my house money in order to cover the court fees. He refused to cancel his trip, however. When I drove him to the airport in Memphis, I asked if he was concerned about how broke we are, but he shook his head. "You're my manager now, so it's your job to worry about that," he said.

First thing every morning, I go out on the porch to feed the dogs and admire my investment. Russ didn't show any surprise when I offered to reimburse the medical school for their commission, nor has he thanked me, but I didn't expect him to. He's moved on already. As for me, I've got calls into half-a-dozen museums and twice as many galleries, both here and in Europe, trying to find a place interested in doing a show. I've been reading back issues of *Artforum*, *ARTnews*, and the like. He claims not to keep up with his profession, the *trends*, he calls them, but that's bullshit. He's got stacks of chronologically-ordered magazines in his workshop. It looks like the Japanese market is hot right now. As soon as I can get the time-difference straight, I'll call some galleries there as well.

In the meantime, junk dealers are coming to haul away his abandoned projects this afternoon. From the designs in his workshop, I can tell he's going to need all the space I can make for his next work. We could both use a clean slate. Besides, in an old *American Art NOW* profile entitled, "I've Seen the Future, and Its Name is Russ Hodges," he said that he didn't believe in the past. A pretentious statement from a pretentious twenty-five-year-old, but I'm trying to follow his words anyway. Except for *Double-Helix*. Before he left for Italy, Russ said, "I should have known that something made from graveyard scrap would end up getting junked."

I'm not so sure. I don't know where it will end up, but every time I look at it, I can't help thinking it has a place somewhere, if I can only find it.

ACKNOWLEDGEMENTS

I would like to thank the editors of the following journals, who published these stories in their original form:

"Dunbar's Folly": *Natural Bridge*

"The Soprano at Midlife": *New Ohio Review*

"Bachelors": *Cimarron Review*

"Shadowboxing": *Buffalo Almanack*

"Good Intentions": *Beloit Fiction Journal*

"Team Players": *Madison Review*

About the Author

Matthew Duffus is the author of the novel *Swapping Purples for Yellows* and the poetry chapbook *Problems of the Soul and Otherwise*. He lives in North Carolina and can be found online at matthewduffus.com and on twitter @DuffusMatthew.

About the Press

Unsolicited Press is a small publisher in Portland, Oregon. The press seeks to produce art, not commodity, from emerging and award-winning authors. Dedicated toward equality in publishing, Unsolicited Press publishes an equal number of men and women each year. Learn more at unsolicitedpress.com and connect with the press on Twitter and Instagram (@unsolicitedpress).